OBLOQUY
By
Amber Geneva

A Symes-Mobberley House Publication

Dedicated to Father

Prologue

Consider this a gentle word of caution. If you have closed your mind to learning new truths, even if they go against everything you've always believed to be fact, read no further. This book is not for you! This is my story. Though it may ruffle more than a few feathers, I am compelled to tell it. And tell it I must!

Chapter One

I married young, at the ripe age of seventeen, right after graduation. My dad was an apostolic minister, and my husband, Greg, was the youth leader with my dad's church.

Mom once had aspirations of my attending a good college after school, doing something with my life other than becoming a minister's wife, like she. Though she didn't say it, I could see it in her eyes – she wasn't happy. It wasn't that she didn't love my dad. I know she did, at first, anyway, but she felt deprived. She wanted more for me – Much more. Wanted me to be independent, if need be. She wanted me to consider the possibility that I might not want to be stuck as a stay-at-home wife and spend my younger years raising a family.

At the time, I promised her that I would consider college and a career. Only that was before Greg Townsend's family moved to San Antonio, where we lived, and joined the church. Greg was thirteen then, and I think I fell in love with his gorgeous green eyes, dark auburn hair, and slightly crooked smile the instant I laid eyes on him.

Greg, on the other hand, didn't seem to really notice me – other than the fact I was the preacher's daughter – for about four years. Then bam! All of a sudden he laid eyes on me one evening during the youth meeting – already, he was teaching the classes under my father's tutelage – I don't know, maybe it was the pretty royal-blue dress Mom had made for me, and maybe not, but as his eyes fell on me when I entered the room a little late, he stopped in midsentence and just stared at me for the longest time, until someone cleared their throat and, embarrassed, he quickly returned to addressing the class. After that, I would catch him watching me when I'd happen to turn his way during church service and youth meetings. I couldn't help but notice that he was definitely interested. To say I was thrilled would be an understatement. I was on the proverbial 'cloud nine'.

Mom noticed too. I could see she was worried. Worried that I might follow in her footsteps and lose what she considered an opportunity to have a real life. She wasn't against my marrying and having a family. She simply wanted me to obtain a college degree of my choosing and have the prospect to have much more.

I told her more than once that I saw no real reason why she couldn't continue her education. She'd shake her head and say it was out of the question. Dad wouldn't like it. He felt that a woman's place was in the home, taking care of family. "But I'm old enough now, Mom," I would argue. "Dad's not an invalid. He can make himself a sandwich once in a while. Get a glass of iced tea." "No," she would reply, "Out of the question." And she would dismiss it at that.

Not fully understanding, one evening I caught Dad at the coffee maker, and Mom was at the store buying groceries for a church dinner the next Sunday, I asked Dad if I could talk to him a minute. Something I rarely did. He always seemed so busy. He wasn't a bad father. He just wasn't a real good one, never seemed available for my minor problems. Not if they couldn't be solved in less than ten minutes. If that was the case, then it was Mom's duty to take care of whatever it was.

"What's up, Kitten?"

"It's Mom."

"Oh! Is she ill?" he inquired, brow wrinkled slightly as he took a momentary seat at the kitchen table.

"No. Not ill. I think she … well …"

"What, Kitten?" He glanced at his watch. "I'm not finished preparing for tomorrow's sermon. I need to get back on it."

"I think she'd like to go to school."

His sudden deeply furrowed frown was immediately followed by a look of incredulity. "No," he said, "you're wrong. Your mother's place is here in the home. There's no job or task more important in a woman's life than taking care of her family; and that goes double for a preacher's wife!" He stood, pretty much in dismissal of what I was trying to get across.

"But she's unhappy!"

Just then, Mom walked in, arms loaded down with groceries. Dad did sit his cup down and ran over and took the sacks for her and placed them on the counter. Mom smiled at me, but her eyes darted back and forth between me and Dad, as she sensed something was going on. "I miss something?"

Dad snorted a laugh. "It's nothing. Brenda has it in her silly head that you're unhappy." He inclined his head back a little. "You're not unhappy, are you?" His mouth twisted around in kind of funny, inquiring quirk.

That was when I saw something I'd never seen before. Something I didn't like. Something in my father's eyes. Why had I never noticed it before?

My father considered himself the master of the house and his word was law! Until that moment – guess I'd been living in ignorant, youthful bliss – I'd believed them pretty much on equal basis. After all, both were my parents. It was kind of a shock to realize that maybe I had perceived it all wrong.

Mom quickly considered me, and I caught a glimpse of something I couldn't recall ever seeing in her eyes before – fear. If it had been there before, I simply hadn't been bright enough to recognize it. I am sure I frowned, not fully understanding, but I was beginning to. Why had I never realized any of this until now?

She was a prisoner! A prisoner of her marriage! A prisoner of her husband! A prisoner of what she had been raised to be proper for a woman!

"Oh my God!" It slipped out before I realized what I said.

Dad snapped his head around. "Excuse me? *What* did you say, young lady?"

I quickly jumped up and muttered, "Nothing. It's nothing." I turned to Mom. "I'm sorry." And I ran off to my room. I think I shook for a good half hour. How could I have been so blind? How could I have not seen it before? Maybe I had just been too young to catch the little innuendos while I was growing up? Perhaps I had been too focused on my own life? My eyes had been opened at last. I was now beginning to understand why my mother was so bent on my attending college. She didn't want me to suffer the same fate as she.

I definitely began to notice things after that. Promised myself that I would not end up like my mother, and when I had the opportunity I let her know that I now understood, for her not to worry about me. The light that came to her eyes then told me I had made her very happy. I didn't want to disappoint her.

*

A year passed, and though I never really forgot the incident in the kitchen with Mom and Dad that day, my focus on what was important had – I hate to admit – altered a great deal. Greg was going to school at the local Christian college to become a minister, and when he wasn't helping Dad, we spent a lot of time together. I was happy and thrilled to simply be aiding Greg in planning lessons – he still taught the youth group – and assisting him with his studies. I had pretty much convinced myself that Greg wasn't like Dad. He understood that a woman needed to be her own person.

Every now and then I would notice Mom's right eye twitching slightly when studying me – something that always happened when she was worried. I understood. But I also convinced myself she was wrong when it came to Greg. Greg wasn't like Dad at all.

I was in love! Blinded by my own stupidity.

Then one late Saturday night, after a week-long revival of which Greg led, he proposed. Like the lovesick idiot I was, I didn't hesitate a second in blurting a voluminous yes. I was ecstatic!

Mom wasn't.

Soon as Greg took me home, we announced our engagement to my folks. I think Mom's mouth dropped a foot. At least, it seemed that way. She was speechless.

Dad, of course, was thrilled and gave us his full blessings. After all, Greg was going to be co-minister of the church soon as he finished his schooling.

The next morning, right before church service – Dad had already left for the church which was just across the yard – Mom knocked on my door.

I opened the door all smiles, happy as I could be. It was clear Mom had been crying. "What's wrong, Mother?" I noticed then that she wasn't dressed for church. Still had on her robe. "Are you sick?"

"I guess I am in a way," she said with unmistakable anger in her tone.

"Are you mad at me?" I knew she wasn't thrilled with me getting married, but I thought she liked Greg. I thought she knew as I did that things would be different with us.

"I am not sure what I am, Brenda. I have spent most of your life trying to insure that you would not make the same mistakes I have."

"I'm not, Mom. I'm not," I tried to assure her.

She rolled her eyes and shook her head despairingly. "You're deluding yourself, young lady. Greg might as well be the carbon copy of your father!"

Angry myself now, I replied, "Mom! How can you say that? He is the sweetest man I've ever known."

She guffawed.

"What's so funny?"

"You really haven't known any men, Brenda. Not really. Greg is the only boy you've ever dated seriously."

"There was Delbert … And Ronnie," I protested.

She chuckled sarcastically again. "Two others besides Greg. Brenda, news flash – That is not nearly enough. You need to get out in the world. You need to find out what you really want out of life. You need to get a college education! You excel in art. Get a degree in art! Granted you probably wouldn't make much unless you were to teach, but that is better than nothing."

"I can marry Greg and still be an artist."

"Maybe you can. And that is a big maybe." She shook her head, flustered. "However, once you're married, you'll probably get pregnant."

"What's wrong with that? I want children."

"Do you seriously think you will have time for art or anything else when you have a tiny baby? And when you're not taking care of that baby, you will have to give your husband all your spare time. I know! I've been there and done that. It's not going to be any different for you."

"You're wrong, Mom! I know you are!" I yelled, now spurting tears too.

Suddenly Dad appeared behind Mom. "What's going on? I can hear you yelling from the church. People are starting to show for service."

Turning quickly on her heels, Mom did something I've never seen her do – she sneered at my father. "Go to hell!" She stormed off.

It is the first time ever that I saw my dad at a complete loss for words.

"She's not happy about my marrying Greg…" was all I could muster. I was so stunned by my mother's behavior.

The next thing I knew, I heard the door to my folk's room slam and my mother stormed back down the hall, dressed in jeans and a sweatshirt, with a backpack thrown over her shoulder. We heard the back door slam and then my mother tearing out of the driveway in her little black Kia Rio.

Dad and I just stood there dumbfounded.

After a moment, Dad's countenance changed from total shock to anger. "She will be sorry she's put on this childish display!" He slapped the wall with his hand and strode out the door and back over to the church.

I didn't know what to do. I just stood there until I heard the back door open again and Greg suddenly came in the hall peering into my room. "Hey there… You okay?"

"I'm not entirely sure."

He stepped in and put his arms around me, trying to comfort me. A gesture that assured me that my mother was wrong about him. I had convinced myself that he was different from my father. After a few minutes, I calmed down and went on over to the church with Greg.

I didn't know it, but I would not see my mother again for a very long time. She didn't come home, nor did she call. It looked more and more like she had left us for good. It took me a while to accept it, but accept it I finally did. At that time, I was actually a little pissed off at her for leaving, especially at such an important time in my life.

Three months later, Greg and I were married in our church, with Dad officiating, of course.

*

The first few weeks were absolute bliss. Greg was on break from school and Dad took over the youth ministry two Wednesdays in a row, giving Greg and me the opportunity to spend a few days on Galveston beach for our honeymoon.

What's more, there was a small guest house on the property with my folks' house, which was included with the church. That's where Greg and I sat up our home.

By the third week, Greg was raring to get back to his youth group and co-pastoring with Dad. I, of course, was right there to support him every step of the way, not even considering that I was doing all the giving and he was doing all the receiving. I was still too blinded by the 'love bug' to see the picture clearly.

Dad, naturally, was happy with me. I'd catch a glimpse of him smiling approvingly at me once in a while. Still, if he did take a minute to ask me how I was doing, he always seemed to get sidetracked by something or someone else. We rarely ever had a conversation with more than one complete sentence. Sometimes not even finishing one.

As more time passed, it was slowly becoming clearer to me what my life was going to be like. That is, unless I took Mom's advice and went back to school. One Wednesday evening after the youth group was over I approached Greg as he was putting away the brown hymnals into the back of the pews. Seeing me coming, he smiled and said, "Good! Would you finish putting these away? Your dad wants to see me about Sunday." He grinned proudly. "He's going to let me deliver the main sermon!" There were no doubts that he was tickled to his toes.

"That's awesome, Greg!"

He swiftly turned to walk away, but I called after him. "There's something I'd like to talk over with you when you are finished."

With a bob of his head, he said, "All right," and went on off to the church office where Dad was.

Only Greg didn't make it to the house until after eleven. At which time, I was already half asleep, and I could see he was tired too. It would have to wait.

Sometime in the middle of the night I began to dream. It wasn't just an ordinary dream that one forgets the minute one awakes. It was much too real. At first I heard a male voice calling my name. The voice was distinct, very masculine, but with a soft, sensual clarity, almost musical. He spoke my name several times before I finally sat up on my elbows, glancing over at Greg, who was sound asleep. There was no way the voice was coming from him. What's more, the voice didn't sound like Greg in the slightest.

"Brenda!" the voice repeated.

I jerked my head around and was stunned by what I saw – the most beautiful man I ever feasted my eyes on! He was tall, stately, with hair that shone of spun gold. His eyes were the most brilliant sky blue, but they had kind of an unusual shape, not exactly human, but he looked human in all other respects. He wore a flowing – silk-like – robe that matched his brilliant eyes, like the ones a person might see in a picture in the Bible. Unable to believe what I was seeing, I was utterly beyond words.

"It's okay, Brenda. I'm not here to harm you. I just want to let you know that I have been watching you for some time."

"What? Why? Who are you? Are you... Are you an angel?"

That seemed to amuse him, as he chuckled casually. My name and who I am is not important at the moment."

"Huh?"

"I just want you to know you are not alone."

Really confused, I asked, "What do you mean? I have a husband. My Dad's just next door."

"Yes," he agreed with a nod. "But are they here for you?"

Not really trusting this strange but gorgeous man – whatever he was – I was hesitant to say much. "Greg and Dad are pastors. They just have a lot to do. It's my place as Greg's wife to help him."

I thought I caught a barely detectable flinch when he said, "What about *you*, though?"

"I ... I ... I'm dreaming. I know this is a dream."

His eyes crinkled in a gentle smile. "Yes you are."

"Then you're not real and I need to wake up."

"Oh ... But I am very real. Just know this, Brenda. I am watching over you. I am here for you if you need me." Then he vanished.

"What?"

Suddenly someone was shaking my shoulders. I opened my eyes to Greg's.

"Brenda! You were talking in your sleep. Are you okay?"

"I just had a really vivid dream."

"Was it a nightmare?"

"No," I answered with hesitance. "I'm not quite sure what it was."

"Well, I suppose that's good. Maybe we can go back to sleep now?"

"Yes. Sleep." I closed my eyes and turned over. But when I did, I suddenly saw those brilliant eyes in my head. I gasped.

"You sure you're okay?" Greg inquired.

"Yeah... Just sneezed," I lied.

That seemed to suffice for Greg. He was instantly back to sleep.

Not me. The man's face was so vivid in my mind that when I got the chance the next afternoon, when Greg and Dad were working together in the church office, I found a clean piece of paper and a pencil in Greg's desk drawer and I drew him. I didn't want Greg to see it though, so I stuck it up in the closet in a shoebox that held some of my mother's photos of me. They didn't hold the same sentimental significance for my father that they did me. So I had kept it. I figured that would be one of the last places Greg would ever look for anything.

*

Right before Greg and I were married, I had secretly gone to the doctor and had him put me on the pill. Something that Dad and Greg both would have frowned on. Still, I guess some of what my mother had tried so hard to instill in me had sunk in. I wanted to wait a while before I let myself get pregnant. Of that, I was glad. For six months later I was coming to realize that I wasn't sure I could handle running errands for Greg, my father, and being in charge of the ladies prayer meeting now on Tuesday afternoons at our home and raising a child too.

Being in charge of the ladies' group really wasn't something I desired to do – not even a little bit – but Greg and Dad insisted that it was my duty (I was really beginning to hate that word at this point) as a pastor's wife to do all I could in supporting the church activities, especially for the women. After all, Mom wasn't there. Therefore, I had to fill her church duties, as well. Another thorn in my side.

I kept telling myself that things would get better, but they never seemed to. One Monday morning Dad received some papers from some lawyer out in Los Angeles – we lived in a suburb of San Antonio – which Mom wanted him to sign. She had filed for divorce.

At first, Dad went about as ballistic as I have ever seen him, snatching up his personal Bible from his desk in his church office and throwing it against the wall, knocking down a framed watercolor of Jesus. Our church didn't look too kindly to divorce. Dad had always preached against it. However, the way he excused his way out of it to the congregation was from the Bible, of course. According to scripture, a man could divorce his wife if she had committed adultery. Therefore, that is what he told the parish the following Sunday morning – That Mom had left him for another man. That she had lost her way and chosen to follow the life of sin. Therefore, God would overlook the divorce. Then he asked the congregation to pray for her sins.

I was sick to my stomach.

To my knowledge, Dad knew no such thing. When he wasn't looking, I chanced to read the papers. They had to do more with property and financial issues than anything. Mom merely stated that Dad had not fulfilled his obligations to her in the marriage and she wanted out. He was neglectful of her needs, and that was putting it mildly, from what I had put together now. Unless he had some other information, he was just assuming he was right and covering his image for the congregation.

On one level, knowing the way my father thought, I could understand his sense of betrayal. However, he refused to see that he had any part in my mother leaving us. His whole life was totally and completely tied up in the church – not his family. In his way of thinking, we should have been grateful that he took care of us at all. That he supported us. It didn't matter that he wasn't there for us as individuals.

More and more I could see why Mom left.

Needless to say, I was beginning to really wish I had listened to her and waited to get married. It was too late, as far as my mother was concerned. However, I now knew that she was in the Los Angeles area. But that covered a lot of territory, about nine million people. And though I did entertain the idea of trying to find her, I knew better than to bring it up to either my husband or my father. I did my best to put the idea out of my head, and tried to do what they expected of me.

But I was growing damn tired of it.

Then Nancy Peloski came to our church with one of our regulars, a matronly widow by the name of Ruth Jamison, her aunt. Nancy wasn't real attractive, kind of plain, and skinny with mousy brown hair and brown eyes.

I, of course, invited Nancy to the ladies' prayer meeting at our house. She hesitated at first, but her aunt insisted that she might enjoy it. So she finally agreed.

Little did I know just how drastically my life was about to change.

Chapter Two

That Tuesday afternoon, right before the women were due to arrive, Greg and I got in a minor argument. He wanted me to run some errands for him after the prayer meeting, and I was already feeling burdened to the max. I politely informed him that I had to cook dinner after the meeting was over and asked him why he couldn't do it. Something I'd never done before.

I have to say that I was a little startled by what I considered overreaction. I saw right away that he was furious. The look on his face almost frightened me. In fact, it brought to mind the day I had seen my Mom react to Dad with fear.

Was I now becoming my mother?

Fortunately for me the doorbell rang, and I went to answer it. It was Nancy, but her aunt didn't come. Nancy said Ruth had a migraine and would have to pass.

I had left Greg standing at the kitchen door that looked out into our little living room. His face was still flushed with anger when I let Nancy in. He did stifle his anger for Nancy's sake, but I could see it wasn't over yet. He bid Nancy hello with a polite smile and then turned to me. "Get those errands done!"

Without further ado he quickly left, passing the other women now filing into our living room.

Nancy definitely noticed. She was shorter than I by about three inches. She turned her brown eyes up to me and whispered, "You okay?"

"I'm not really certain," I replied.

She glanced around at the other women who were taking their seats in the chairs we had placed in a circle in the living room, Bibles in their laps, and then turned back to me. "Hey... If you ever need to talk, I'm all ears."

"Thanks! Maybe I will."

She smiled pleasantly and took her seat.

I retrieved my Bible from the end table, along with my notes and went to the middle of the circle to lead the group in an opening prayer. Something that I definitely did not feel like doing.

I could tell Nancy was bored out of her gourd, as the old saying goes. However, she came the next week too. I did notice that she was wearing long sleeves both times, and it had to be ninety plus outside. Of course we had air conditioning, but the other girls in the group, and even the older ladies, all wore short sleeves.

So, I took it upon myself the second Tuesday afternoon when we were taking a refreshment break to just come right and ask her. I stepped up to the coffee machine and poured myself a cup, sweetened it and turned to her, as she was helping herself to some fruit punch. "Your red blouse is really pretty, but aren't you hot in those long sleeves?"

She took a sip of her drink and blushed before sitting her glass aside. Then in almost a whisper, she replied, "Tattoos. I have tattoos."

"Oh!" I felt kind of sorry I had asked. It had not been my intention to embarrass her, but by her expression, I surely had.

"Aunt Ruth informed me that the church frowns upon them. That's why I'm wearing long sleeves."

I indicated with a vague nod that she was correct. "Yes. The Bible is pretty clear about one not getting tattoos. But hey… Once you turn to Christ, it will be forgiven." I thought surely that my telling her that she would be forgiven she would feel better about it.

That was hardly the impression I received though.

Instead, she responded with, "Hmmm … That doesn't really hit me right."

Confused myself, I inquired, "But you'll be forgiven?"

Her tone changed to slightly sarcastic. "What? What I do to my body? The clothes I wear? Makeup? All that can be considered sinful? I see the women here wear little if any makeup. I thought it was what was in a person's heart, not what they wore or did to their own bodies that made them good?"

"Yes! Of course, you have a valid point. But the Bible—."

She put out a hand. "Hey! It's okay. I'm only here to humor my aunt." She took another sip of her punch, eyeing me over the brim of her glass, pondering something. She set the glass aside and said, "Between you and me," she said, glancing off at the others as she spoke in a low tone, "I can see you're not happy. In fact, you're miserable! So why on Earth would you want to pass that on to someone else?"

She had me. In an instant, she had changed from what I had believed to be an unassuming young woman to a girl who clearly knew what she wanted.

And it wasn't church.

"I... I'm sorry. I guess I thought you were here for the Lord."

She turned to walk away.

"Wait... please," I said.

She swung back around.

"I like you, Nancy. And – Yes..." I lowered my voice then. "You're right. I am miserable."

Her eyes lit up and a gratified grin spread across her freckle-sprinkled face. "I like you too."

She went over to the chair she'd been sitting in and snatched up her small purse, took out a card and gave it to me. "My number and address, if you ever decide *you* want to change your life for the better."

I'm sure my eyes were saucers of surprise by her statement. I tentatively took the card and thanked her.

"You're welcome. And, I won't be coming to these meetings anymore. However, I have a group of friends of my own whom I would love to introduce you too. We meet once a month."

"I'll definitely consider it," I replied, wondering where this was leading, if anywhere.

She grinned as though pleased and returned to her seat. It was then that I realized the ten minutes of break time had gone into twenty. I apologized to the rest of the women and went back to leading the women in their lesson for the day.

Of course, Dad and Greg kept me way too busy to even think much about what had transpired between Nancy and me. I literally felt like they were trying to run me to death: cooking for special Sunday night dinners every fifth Sunday – of course others brought dishes as well – but being a pastor's wife, I had to furnish the main course. There was the Tuesday afternoon gatherings, and then visiting sick folks in the hospital and nursing homes at least one day a week. That didn't include my regular chores of buying our own groceries, cooking our own meals, and fulfilling my 'wifely' duties for Greg.

There had been a time when I desired him beyond belief, and at first he had taken the time for a certain amount of foreplay. After almost a year of being married, though, it was pretty much cut down to his being satisfied, and my being so tired with everything else, that I really didn't care much that I was left high and dry and sexually frustrated.

It hit me one afternoon when I was out shopping for church supplies that – aside from the fact that I didn't have a baby to care for – I had not one but two very demanding men to care for. What's more, they totally expected it of me. Without question, they considered it my duty!

I think I stopped in my tracks then. I was in Costco in front of a big display of diapers. The longer I stood there and thought about it, the more it hammered home to me –

I was a fool!

"Oh dear God! Mom, how could I be so blind?"

Not only had I not listened to her and made a life of misery for myself, I was doing double-time. I literally had no life of my own!

Right then and there I opened my purse and searched for Nancy's card. I breathed a sigh of relief when I found it stuck in a slot in my wallet. "Thank you! Thank you!"

I realized that a middle-aged Hispanic woman was staring at me strangely.

I smiled at her and said, "Thought I lost it. Friend's phone number."

She smiled back and continued on with her shopping.

I wasn't sure how I was going to get away from Dad and Greg long enough to do much of anything that wasn't directly connected with the church and family. I was desperate though and had to think of something. After some consideration and thought, I realized that I could tell Greg that I wanted to pay a visit to a possible new parishioner. I made the point of reminding him that she was the niece of Ruth Jamison. Did he remember her?

At first, he didn't.

I pressed the issue though. Told him that I thought she needed spiritual guidance. Actually I was the one who needed a spiritual uplifting.

Finally, he recalled her coming to church with Ruth. "Oh! Yes. I remember now," he said. "The girl with mousy brown hair and freckles."

"Yes! She's the one."

He blew out air. "Well, okay. Since it's for a good cause, I suppose we can spare you for a bit. Just don't forget to print up the church pamphlets for Sunday morning service."

I walked out the door that evening and peered up at the star-filled sky. For the first time in I couldn't remember when I felt a taste of freedom. Yes! Wonderful blessed freedom! I felt as though a huge weight had been lifted from my shoulders, at least, for a few hours.

I have to admit that I was kind of shocked when Nancy opened the door. The lights had been turned off, but candles were lit everywhere. There were four other your women in the room. Rebecca with long blonde hair in braids – looked Scandinavian, Maggie with short black hair and big dark eyes, Lisa with wavy red hair to her shoulders, and Char with chestnut hair and hazel eyes. All the girls wore necklaces with silver stars and Char had a tattoo of a woman that looked Egyptian on her right arm. Under it was the name Isis.

I have to admit that I was a bit ignorant of witchcraft, but right away I knew that something strange was going on. Having lived a much sheltered church life, I instantly felt out of place.

Nancy knew right away that I was uncomfortable. She smiled supportively up to me and said, "Now you know how I feel when I am in your church."

"You're… You're …"

"Wiccan's," Char replied. "We are witches."

"I'm sorry," I said, suffering momentary panic. "This was a big mistake. I should go." I turned to walk back out.

"No! No! No!" Nancy quickly replied. "I suffered through your church services and classes a couple of times. The least you can do is find out what we are really about." She skewed her head inquisitively to the right. "You have to admit it's only fair."

All the women stood around me. They were determined. Of that, I had no doubt.

I stuttered. "I… I… I… Greg will kill me. And so will my father. I can't be here!

Rebecca, the tallest one with braids spoke, "Oh yes you can! We can prove to you that all you've been taught through the years is nothing but bull!"

"What?" I was not only incredulous now, I felt insulted. "How dare you!"

Nancy didn't hesitate to get in my face. "Just give us five minutes, Brenda. Please!" she pleaded, voice softening.

I was scared. I had no idea what to expect.

"You're not happy," Nancy said. "You admitted to me that you aren't. So give yourself a chance to learn what your right to know is."

"All right," I said. "Five minutes."

Rebecca spoke again, "Did you know that the original story of Noah was taken from The Epic of Gilgamesh? That there are stories of a flood in many of the world's mythologies? Noah is not original!"

Then Char piped up, "Did you know that Isis' worshipers had to be baptized? Baptism did not originate with Christianity!"

"What? No! You're wrong!" I insisted.

"No we're not!" Nancy replied. "We can show you."

Maggie spoke up for the first time. She held a big Bible in her hand. The first half was written in Hebrew and the second in English. There were notes at the bottom of the pages as well. She proceeded to point a finger to a passage in Genesis. "Look here, Brenda. Have you ever wondered why it says gods here? Why is it plural?"

"Oh…" I said, familiar with the scripture and repeating what I'd heard my father say, "It just means the heavenly court."

"No! That's not what it means at all," Brenda insisted. "It means there is more than one god."

"To put it simply," Char interjected, "the Jews took the mythologies of the world, slapped Jewish names on the characters and credited the stories as their own, wanting the world to believe that they were the *chosen* race."

I felt like I was under some kind of attack. It was all too much too quick. I shook from head to foot. I realize now, though, that they knew I would not sit down and simply listen. They had to throw as much at me as they could while they had the chance. I had no idea where all this was coming from and was in no way prepared for what I was hearing. "No! You've got to be wrong!"

Nancy gently took my hand. "Hey… It's up to you whether you want to learn the truth or not. Not saying we have all the answers, but what you have been raised to believe all your life is… basically… lies!"

"Just do some research, Brenda," Char interjected.

"I can see you are upset," Rebecca stated. "But you have a right to know the truth. Don't take our word for it. Research what we're telling you."

"You have a computer, don't you?" Nancy asked.

"Yes…"

"Then look up the works of James Frazier and Robert Graves, to name a few. There are more. What you have been taught is all lies."

"But what about Jesus?" I threw in, not sure what to say now. Nancy replied, "I personally believe he was a teacher, a very enlightened guru, possibly. He did stand up to the Jews. What's more, he never really claimed to be the son of God. He referred to himself as the son of man."

I thought about it a minute. "I couldn't recall Jesus ever saying he was the only son of God. However, there were passages that could be construed that way. "Okay," I said, more to appease them than anything. "I'll research what you've said."

"Good!" Nancy replied. "That's all we ask. But don't rush it. Take your time. It took me a while to realize the truth. Because of all the years of conditioning, it takes time to see the truth even when it is right smack in your face."

"Okay," I replied. "Okay. I promise to look into it." I turned to go then, and Rebecca opened the door for me.

Nancy said, "You're always welcome, Brenda. If you decide you want to come back, give me a call."

"Okay. I will. Thanks… I think." I left with a headache. I had no earthly idea what to think.

I was so upset that I drove around for half an hour before returning home. Besides, I hadn't been gone that long, and Greg would know things didn't go well if I went home too soon.

I kept thinking about all the things the girls had thrown at me. "They can't be right," I assured myself. "They have to be wrong."

Suddenly my mother's face came to mind. I thought of all the things she had tried to instill in me and the things that she had questioned all her life. She always said that something just didn't feel right. That a truly loving God would not treat women as second-rate, that they would be equal with men.

Another thing she had questioned was the fact that one could pray and pray and pray and often it was as though God either never heard, or, if He did, He didn't care. Of course, my Dad's answer to that was simple – If it isn't God's will, then it isn't God's will. It isn't going to happen.

My father, as so many other preachers I had heard over the years when they had come as guest ministers, insisted that God's word was infallible. Well, if that were true, why were there so many inconsistencies? The Old Testament would say one thing, but Jesus would say something to the contrary in the New Testament. Why was that? I had to admit, the young pagan women had set me to thinking. However, I was too shook up right then to do anything about it. I merely went home and did my best to make myself appear as though all had gone well.

I'm not entirely certain that Greg bought my charade, but he didn't question me. I did my best to put on a happy face. It was bedtime, but I hadn't forgotten the fliers. I told him that I would run take care of them while he took his shower and dressed for bed. That seemed to satisfy him, so off I went to the church office to print up the fliers.

While there in the office, I happened to glance over at the somewhat extensive library my father had amassed over the years. As I scanned over the titles, I noticed something that had never hit home to me before, although I had seen those books thousands of times. They weren't just books on Christianity. Father had books on numerous mythologies from what I could see.

I even saw a book on *The Golden Bough*. I took it out and flipped through the pages. It wasn't the work itself, from what I understood. It was a commentary from a 'Christian' perspective, of course. There were books on the ancient Egyptians, on their gods, and Dad even had one that focused on Isis. I grabbed it off the shelf and glanced through it. And low and behold, if I didn't come across a paragraph where it spoke of baptism. The girls had told me the truth! Baptism did *not* originate with Christianity!

I stuck the book back in its allotted slot. My mind was reeling now. I knew that most of the books Dad had would be influenced by Christian thinking. I needed to go to the library to do my research. There I should be able to find books written by folks with more, unbiased minds. "Yes!" I told myself. "The next time I had to run to the store, I would stop at the library and see what they had to offer.

By the time I was done with printing up the pamphlets and back to the house, Greg was asleep. Of that, I was thankful. I really wasn't in any mood to talk to him. What's more, I was especially not in the mood to have unfulfilled sex.

A week passed before I found the opportunity to visit our local library. Immediately, I went to one of the available terminals and looked up *The Golden Bough.* They had it okay. From what I could glean, the original work was in two volumes, later in three, and then finally in twelve. "Gee!" I said to myself. "I wonder if they have all twelve?" They did carry all of them, but most were checked out to other folks. There were three volumes available though: Numbers one, four, and five. I knew I wouldn't have time to read all three before they would be due back. And I thought if I could at least read number one that maybe two would be in when I went back. So, I eagerly checked it out, figuring it was as good a start as any.

Finding a time to read it wasn't the only problem. Where to hide it, was one as well. I had intentionally taken my larger purse, and was able to stick the book inside. And when Greg was otherwise occupied, I took the book out and slipped it in the bathroom closet behind my feminine products, thinking that Greg probably wouldn't be looking there. That way, I could hide in the bathroom and read when they were busy working on sermons and such.

It took a while, but I finally managed to get through the book, and was eager to check out another, for I was now fully convinced that the Wiccan girls had told me the truth. It seemed that it was definitely a good possibility that I had been raised on a lie.

I'm not saying that God isn't real or doesn't exist. Just saying that what I had been taught wasn't exactly the truth; that all was very questionable to say the very least. My interest had been thoroughly piqued.

I managed to finish the book in just under the two weeks that I had it for. Anxious to get another soon as I had the opportunity, I took it back. However, I was disappointed. For all the volumes had been checked out. I decided that surely there was something else. I scanned over the titles and came across several interesting books by other authors such as: Archarya S and Robert Graves. And there were some I wasn't sure of, but decided that I would check them out later, if need be. For then, though, I grabbed *The White Goddess* by Robert Graves.

I ended up having to renew *The White Goddess*. There was so much information in it that it made my head spin. But that wasn't the only thing that was throwing me off kilter. I was blown away from what I had learned and was learning. I could not believe that the public had all this information available to them, but a good majority of the populace either didn't know it existed, or were afraid to examine.

I was literally in a state of shock.

It must have shown to an extent, for one afternoon after Greg was through going over some plans for the next service with my father, Greg came up behind me while I was cooking dinner.

He put his arms around me from behind. Something he had not done in a while. "You okay?" he asked.

I was surprised that he even asked. "Yeah. Sure," I turned and faced him. "Why do you ask?"

"You just seem withdrawn lately. You're not sick, are you?"

I told him I was okay and turned back to stir the spaghetti sauce.

He gently took hold of my wrist and made me turn around and look at him. "Brenda, something is going on with you. What is it?"

I sniggered faintly.

"Something funny?"

He was being really nice, for once. I didn't want to ruin it. "No. It's just… Well, I'm not used to you noticing me."

"What?" Immediately he looked hurt.

I apologized and told him that that hadn't come out right.

"No! You're right, Brenda. I haven't paid much attention to you lately. I've been so tied up with everything else."

"I won't argue that. But I understand."

"Do you really? Honestly, I'm not sure I do anymore."

This surprised me. "Huh? What are you saying?"

"I had a weird dream last night. I dreamed you left me for this really... well... very good-looking blond-headed man."

"Blond-headed man?" I questioned, suddenly remembering my own dream. "What?"

"It was so real. I woke up in a sweat. I looked over at you, but you were sleeping so peacefully, I didn't want to disturb you. I have to admit, though, that it did unglue me." He pulled me close and kissed the crown of my head. "I love you, Brenda! I don't want to ever lose you."

Now I was thrown for another loop. Just when I was thinking I was going to end up bailing out on my family the way Mom did, Greg had to go throw his monkey wrench into the works.

I looked up at him as sweetly and convincingly as I could, and said, "I have no plans to go anywhere, Greg." I actually meant it at that moment.

He pulled back, locking his eyes on mine. "You're absolutely sure?"

"There's no one but you, Greg. But I will be honest, sometimes I feel like I'm just a tool for you and Daddy to use... running all the errands, doing all the cooking, backing you and Daddy up all the time on basically everything. I have to ask myself, who is going to back me up?"

"I will! I'm your husband! I realize that I have been so caught up in the church that I have neglected you. For that, I am genuinely sorry. But that's all going to change right now. I promise!"

At that moment, I began to feel guilty for what I had been doing the past few weeks. And my heart once more went out to my husband. He did love me. It was there in his eyes. He kissed me ever so tenderly and when he pulled away, he took the spoon and placed it aside. "The sauce has to cook for a while, doesn't it?"

I bobbed my head yes.

His eyes brightened. "Dad's on the phone with some other pastor. They're arguing over dogma, believe it or not."

"Seriously?"

"Seriously." A familiar glint came to his eyes. One I hadn't seen in a while. "Our dinner can wait. Let's go have some 'us' time for a few minutes. Want to?"

I was a bit surprised, but right now he was being the man I had fallen in love with. "Yes!" I emphasized with a nod.

He scooped me up in his arms and carried me to our bedroom. He then made love to me in the most considerate and gentle fashion. It was even more wonderful than had been on our honeymoon. Afterwards, we lay in one another's arms for a while, that is until we heard Dad calling to us from the kitchen.

Greg laughed, and I giggled.

He jumped out of bed, opened our bedroom door and told Dad that we'd be out in a few minutes. Then he grabbed my hand and we took a quick shower together.

When done, Greg dressed and ran on out to see Dad. I, of course, took a little longer. I put my dark brown hair up in a bun since it was wet. Five minutes later, I was heating the water for the spaghetti.

Chapter Three

Greg kept his promise for about a month, but Dad kept pressuring him for this and that, and when it came right down to it, I know Greg considered God first and, of course, over his wife. Things went back to almost exactly the way they had been. However, once in a great while Greg would stop long enough to give me a hug and a kiss on the cheek, tell me he loved me, and then out the door and over to the church he'd go.

I appreciated the little gestures. I knew he loved me. But he loved God and church more. Which in some ways might by many seem okay, considering the way we had been brought up to believe, but I was once again feeling abandoned and already pulling a heavy load with my own duties, not even including all the numerous errands I ran for my two pastors.

Life was grueling to say the least.

I hadn't completely forgotten about the library books. I kept returning them and checking out more, but I barely had time to glance at them, let alone, read them. Then one day it happened –

Greg found them!

I was in the laundry room loading the washer when I heard, *"Brenda!"*

At first I thought he was hurt, he yelled so loud. I dashed out of the laundry room to find him standing in the bathroom door, a book in each hand, shaking them angrily at me.

"What … In God's name is this?"

"Ah …" I stuttered. "I really had believed he never would find them. Not fully thinking with all my brains, I stupidly asked, "Where did you get those?"

"You know where I got them, Brenda!" he angrily retorted. "Behind your feminine products! I was looking for toilet paper, and look what I found!"

"The toilet paper is under the sink," I replied as calmly as I could.

He sat the books on the toilet seat and rudely stuck a palm in my face. "Don't! Don't even try to shrug this off as nothing. You and I are the only two people living here. And your father is the only person who might come in our bathroom. God knows I didn't put them there... and neither did your dad!" He seemed to be making an effort to calm down, taking in a couple of deep breaths before speaking again. "Please tell me why you would read such garbage?"

That was when I pointed out that there were all kinds of books on mythologies and other religions in Dad's library.

He shook his head so hard it vibrated. "Not the same thing! Those books are there only for reference, Brenda. So your father and I can counteract anything anyone tries to propose as a valid argument."

"I kind of get that, Greg. But the library books have been written by noted scholars – famous men and women. They have worked years and years on researching them. I am just looking for the truth!"

"You have the truth!" he yelled. "Jesus Christ is your savior. And anything else is of the devil!"

I had always known that Greg and Dad were really set in their beliefs, but it wasn't until that moment that I understood just how set Greg was. "Oh my God!" It slipped out. I couldn't help it.

"Don't!" he yelled again, face red, perspiring now. I thought he was going to have a stroke. *"You do not take the Lord's name in vain, Brenda! And don't you ever bring such trash into our home again! Is that understood?"*

Dad suddenly appeared in the room. "Thought I heard yelling," he said, eyes going back and forth between me and Greg.

Greg handed the books over to my dad.

Dad took one look at them and was instantly slack jawed. He just stared at the titles for a minute, and then turned each book over to look at the backs, and then back again. Then he focused his stare on me. "Brenda! What is the meaning of this? How could you?"

Really angry now and feeling more defensive than I'd ever felt in my life, I hotly replied, "Easy! I'm tired of being treated like you are treating me now! Like I am some kind of imbecile who can't think for herself! Tired of being treated like an ignorant slave!"

Both frowned, staring at me in disbelief.

"You're not a slave, Brenda," Dad said.

"Oh *yes* I am! I am a slave to a religion that I'm not sure I really believe in anymore."

"Brenda!" Dad was beside himself, shaking violently.

I took a good look at the both of them, and suddenly I felt sorry for them. I did love them, but I didn't love all the rules and strict obedience to a religion that I had serious doubts about. "I'm sorry, Dad… Greg," I finally said. "But I just wanted to know the truth. And I see absolutely nothing wrong with that. I really would be an idiot if I didn't want to know." I turned and stormed out of the house, for I too trembled violently and had to get out of there.

I didn't even bother to grab my car keys, but my small change purse with my bank card sat on the coffee table. I grabbed it and stuck it in my back pocket, where I already had my cell phone.

I had on jeans, a red tee-shirt, and tennis shoes. I took off running, running as fast as I could. Dad and Greg both called to me, but I ignored them. There was no solution to the argument. So, I saw no point in continuing it.

There was a park a few blocks down. I ran and ran until I reached it, found a bench away from the street that was behind some trees and collapsed there. I didn't want Greg or my dad to find me.

I was grateful that there weren't many people in the park, for I desperately needed to be alone. I did see a tall young man with blond hair not far from me feeding peanuts to some squirrels. He was dressed in jogging attire and I thought nothing of it.

I let the tears flow. And flow they did. I must have cried hard for ten minutes, burying my head in my hands on my lap.

"Are you okay, Brenda?" a pleasant male voice inquired.

I glanced up into the handsome face with kind blue eyes. At once, he reminded me of the man I had had in the dream not too long ago. But he didn't look exactly like the man in my dream. "Do I know you?" I quickly tried to wipe the tears from my face with my bare hands.

He handed me a clean tissue. "Always carry them," he said, smiling politely. "…Allergies," he explained.

"Oh! Ok… thanks!"

"Please forgive me for my intrusion, but you looked as though you could use a friend."

Suddenly I remembered that he had called me by my name. "How did you know my name? Have you been to my Dad's church?"

"I've dropped in a time or two."

"Oh! I don't remember ever seeing you there."

"I definitely remember you. You're always up at the front with you dad and husband. I tend to hang back." He gestured with his hand to the bench. "May I?"

"Certainly."

He eased down beside me. I smiled into his fine, chiseled face. That was when I noticed that his eyes had a strange slant. The same slant as the man in my dream. I trailed my own eyes across his face. He was really fair. What's more, he had no blemishes of any kind that I could tell. Flawless as a newborn baby. Only, there was a maturity about him that defied his youthful appearance.

I was going to ask him what his name was when he said, "I'm Erick, by the way."

"Erick, huh? Not sure I've ever known anyone personally by that name before. Of course, I've heard it."

"Not as common as some maybe."

Just his being beside me had an amazing calming effect. I almost forgot how upset I had been.

"Do I detect a smile?" he inquired with a most captivating grin.

"Wasn't aware that I was," I commented with surprise.

"Much better than all those tears of anguish."

I realized then that I definitely was smiling. Who was this amazing man? I looked into those strange but oh so beautiful eyes, and could have easily got lost in them, but was rudely brought back to the harsh reality of my family.

"Brenda!" Greg called from behind.

I snapped my head around to see my husband running towards me, and my father not too far behind. I turned to my friend – but he wasn't there! "What the—?"

Then I could swear I heard his voice, clear as a bell in my head, "Don't worry, Brenda. I'm still around."

Something strange was happening. Where did he go? Greg reached me, and then Dad, but I no longer felt the anguish I had only ten minutes before, for I knew I had a friend; possibly a very *special* friend. That gave me the strength to do whatever it was that I needed to do.

"I just had to get away," I said, speaking with amazing calm and actually smiling up at the two very perplexed men in my life.

"You need to come home with us right now, young lady!" Dad said with his authoritarian voice.

I stood and faced him. "I'm *not* a child, Dad! You do not speak to me that way. You treat me with respect!" His jaw dropped. I turned to Greg. "The same goes for you! I am *not* your slave! I am a grown woman and I deserve the same respect as anyone. Just because you two are ministers of your chosen faith, doesn't give you the right to treat me like some second-class citizen. You treat me as an equal – Or I am out of here! Is that understood?"

Both were speechless momentarily, as I took off walking very fast back to the house.

A minute later, Greg caught up to me. "Brenda... I know you're upset right now. But this behavior of yours is unacceptable!"

I faced him squarely. "I am defending my rights as a human being! If you have a problem with that, get a divorce!" And I took off running; not because I was upset. I just felt like running. It felt good. I felt good! I loved my husband and my dad, but I also loved myself! Had I listened to Mom, none of this would be happening right now. And where was she? I hoped that she would come home someday.

Greg and Dad didn't try to keep up with me. For one thing, I believe they were both exhausted. I just went in the house and continued loading the laundry in the washing machine. I did hear them come in shortly and go in mine and Greg's bedroom, more than likely to discuss me.

I made myself fresh coffee and took it with me to the front porch and sat down on the bottom step. I half expected them to come out, but they didn't. After a bit, I heard the back door slam and knew they were heading over to the church. I thought, hoped, that maybe they understood that there was no arguing with me.

A week passed with the three of us barely speaking to one another, and then only when necessary. I went ahead and did the women's meeting on Tuesday afternoon, ran the errands and did the chores. What's more, I took the books back to the library. But it had nothing to do with Dad and Greg demanding me to.

I didn't need them anymore.

I knew there was something more, something I felt sure wasn't written about in any mainstream publications that I knew of, and maybe not in any. And if it was, it was well-hidden and little publicized.

I hadn't seen Erick anymore, but he had promised that he would be close, and for some crazy reason I believed him.

I did, however, decide to pay Nancy a visit one afternoon. She worked at Baskin Robbins. It was hot, and I thought it a good day for ice cream, as well. So I dropped in. She seemed a little surprised to see me, but smiled as she waited on a teenage boy with spiked red hair first. When she was done, I told her I wanted two scoops of coffee ice cream. She handed it over, and I paid for it. Then I apologized for the way I had behaved that night at her house.

The teen had left and there was only an elderly couple sitting at a table on the far side. She rinsed off the ice cream scooper and set it aside and then looked up at me. "It's okay, Brenda. I understand. It takes a while for people to change when they've been so conditioned all their lives to believe something, even when it isn't true." She leaned in just over the glass top. "I know. It took me a while. But I couldn't be happier now. Wicca is where I belong. And Wicca is where I'm going to stay!"

"When is your next meeting?"

"On the full moon. We always meet on the full moon and other pagan holidays."

"Oh?"

She held up a forefinger. "Just a sec." She pulled her purse out from under the side counter, took out a slip of paper and handed it over. "I just happened to have this in my purse. It's a calendar of our events for the next six months. Take it. I have extras."

"Oh! Thank you!" I took it eagerly and stuck it in my back pocket. I headed out the door with a great feeling. Hopefully, in Wicca I would find the spiritual happiness I'd been so desperately searching for.

Where would I hide it that no one would find it? Then it hit me – the church piano! No one ever looked inside the church piano. Soon as I arrived home, after making sure Dad and Greg were busy in the office, I looked over the schedule quickly, memorizing as much as I could, folded it down as small as I possibly could, and then I slipped quietly into the church and lifted the lid to the black baby grand and stuck it down in the bottom of the piano, under the strings. I felt sure no one would find it there.

I had piano lessons as a child and often played for services. Something else expected of me when the other pianist, George Fontaine, couldn't make it. To make sure the paper wouldn't interfere with the action of the keys, I sat down and played a couple of hymns.

I must not have been thinking, for Dad and Greg both suddenly stood beside me, all smiles. Apparently they thought I was having an uplifting moment and realizing that I had been in error of my ways. I smiled back at them, not indicting otherwise.

"Sounds lovely," Greg complimented. "Are you thinking of playing a piece for Sunday service?"

"You want me to?" I asked, evading the question.

Dad was pleased and said, "It would be wonderful."

"I can do that." I put the hymnal away in the bench and stood. "I guess I should get ready for the ladies' group," I said, glancing at the time on my wristwatch.

Smiling very pleased, Greg kissed my cheek. I smiled back and waltzed out of the church. Maybe I should have felt guilty, but I didn't. I saw no way where I could be completely honest with them, for they had made it clear that such an attempt would be impossible. I knew what I had to do.

*

I actually managed to get out of the house without question the next full moon. Almost weekly, many of the women in our church would make hospital visits to members who were ill. Nearly always there was at least one elderly gentleman or lady sick. I had gone a few times in the past, but decided that I would start again – at least on the nights of the full moon when Nancy's group held their meetings. And I did go, but I would only stay a few minutes, excusing myself to the girls I was with, telling them I was going to visit some folks on another floor, and then when I felt the coast was clear I would leave.

I was especially nervous at first, letting Nancy initiate me, but I soon got the hang of things, quickly learning how to draw the nine-foot circle and blessing the corners. It wasn't long before Nancy let me lead the group in order to get the feel of things.

I was elated!

The energy I felt at the end of each ritual was unbelievable. I felt I had found my truth. I was ecstatic!

Only I never saw Erick once during all this, nor did I have any more dreams. I was beginning to wonder if I had imagined Erick, being as distraught as I had been that day.

All went well for the next three months. I was so happy with my new religion and my new life, that I didn't mind doing my church and wifely duties so much. It was still hard, but having something to look forward to made it all bearable. I often dropped by Baskin Robbins to visit with Nancy during the day, knowing my dad and Greg wouldn't think anything of me getting myself an ice cream cone. It was perfect.

But nothing lasts forever.

After only three months it all went south. I left Nancy's that last full moon and went straight home, as always. It wasn't real late, but visiting hours at the hospital had been over for almost an hour; definitely time I should have been home.

I thought all was okay and was feeling really good from the ritual, all energized and happy. I let myself in the front door, expecting Greg to be either studying for the next Sunday's sermon or getting ready for bed. He wasn't in the house, so I went on to the bathroom, that was just off our bedroom, to shower and get ready for bed, assuming Greg was with Dad. All of a sudden, I heard the front door bang open and Dad and Greg charging in the house. "What the—?" I turned to see both standing in the bedroom doorway looking angry – very, very angry!

"What's going on?" I asked, really unsure of what was happening.

"Where have you been, Brenda?" Dad asked, and in not too kind of a voice.

"You know. I went to the hospital."

"After that?" Greg piped in.

"What do you mean? What are you talking about?" I asked, now definitely feeling more than a little anxious.

Dad informed me that Ruth Jamison had come by earlier, while I was supposed to be at the hospital. Doing my best to remain calm, I asked, "What did she want?"

"First of all," Greg said, "her niece Nancy is a witch! She had brought her to church hoping to save her soul, but it didn't work. Nancy's still practicing witchcraft."

Frowning more than uncomfortably, I said, "What has that to do with me?"

"You know good and well, Brenda!" Greg shouted. "You've been going over there instead of the hospital."

"I have been going to the hospital. Just ask the girls."

"You go," Dad said. "But you don't stay. We talked to the other ladies. All tell us that you say you are going to visit patients on another floor and they don't see you anymore."

Greg added, "That's because you're going to Nancy's!"

I opened my mouth to speak, but wasn't sure what I was going to say, but Dad spoke instead, "We got her address from Ruth. We followed you from the hospital tonight, and sure enough, you went straight to that address!"

Dad, eyes tearful, practically screamed, "You've been practicing witchcraft, Brenda! How could you do such a thing?"

I was torn. I felt for my dad, but I was also angry at the ignorance I faced. "Dammit!" I swore shocking them even more, "There is something called freedom of religion in this country!"

"That may be so, Brenda," Dad replied, now managing to contain his tears. "But you were raised under a Christian roof! By a Christian preacher! You even married a pastor! What on God's green Earth is wrong with you?"

"I am tired of living a lie!" I screamed. *"I searched for the truth! There is nothing wrong with that!"*

Suddenly there was a hard blow to my left jaw and I flew backwards across the room, landing hard on my butt. I was so stunned I couldn't see straight for a moment.

Greg rushed up, and for a brief second I thought he was checking to see if I was hurt.

I thought wrong.

He grabbed both my wrists and Dad grabbed my feet and they carried me out of the house and across the yard, heading for the church.

"What are you doing?" I was truly scared now for the first time in my life. Scared of my own father and husband!

Adding to the horror, as they carried me into the church, I had the awful realization that the church was full! They had called in all the members. And Ruth Jamison sat smugly on the front pew. I screamed, "Bitch!" And promptly was slapped, this time, by Greg.

All too quickly I realized they were going to perform an exorcism on me – an exorcism! I screamed for them to let me go. I pleaded. I was never so humiliated, angry, hurt and embarrassed in my entire life. I just wanted to die.

Everyone gathered in a circle around me, praying and raising their hands, while Greg tied my hands behind my back and sat me in a chair. Dad had his Bible and began quoting scripture after scripture.

"I haven't done anything wrong!" I yelled, now crying.

Greg told me to confess my sins and beg Jesus for forgiveness.

Again, I insisted that I hadn't done anything wrong. What's more, I didn't believe I had.

Then all of a sudden something dark, like a miniature cloud, shot through the air. I thought I was just imagining it, but then there was another, and then another. From what I could figure out, they were giving the church members electrical shocks; frightening them out of their wits, of course. Many of the members fled out the doors.

Dad glared down at me and demanded I make the spirits stop.

"I can't!" I had no idea what they were. There was no way I could make them stop. What's more, I was beginning to doublethink what I had done. Maybe… Just maybe I was in the wrong?

One zapped Greg good, sent him lunging back across a front pew.

"Make them stop!" Dad shrieked, terror in his eyes.

"I don't know how!" I didn't know what else to do. I cried out for Jesus to forgive me. I think I must have screamed it ten times or more.

Then the clouds disappeared just as quickly as they had come.

What few church members who had remained stood around in shock, as well as Dad and Greg.

I think I was hit the hardest by it all.

I felt totally betrayed – And totally the fool.

Satisfied, at last, Dad and Greg released me from my bonds. Greg led me out of the church and towards home, while Dad stayed back to speak to the members there.

I don't believe I said ten words all through the next week.

Chapter Four

Life was not the same for me anymore. All faith had gone out the door. I hadn't been happy as a Christian, and yet after I had been consecrated as a Wiccan, I had met an even worse fate.

How could a god, Christian or otherwise, be so cruel? I did my chores, and I performed my duties. However, because of the blemish, as my father put it, I had put on the church, I was no longer allowed – which I was glad – to teach members in any way or form. I wasn't allowed to play the piano for services, and I wasn't allowed to speak up in church.

Conversely, had I stood in front of the entire congregation and declared that I had been deceived and had greatly sinned and begged for not only God's forgiveness, but the members as well, then I would have been allowed to at least play the piano for services and lead a prayer once in a while.

I refused. Part of me stubbornly clung to the fact that maybe I had been right. Maybe the dark clouds or whatever they had been had not come because of me.

I did what I had to do and no more.

My hope, my fight, was gone. I didn't give a crap about anything. I was numb inside.

I suppose that deep down I still loved my father and my husband, but at the same time I loathed the fact that they were so high and mighty in their attitudes and opinions of themselves, believing they could do no wrong.

I was more miserable than I had been in my entire life.

When I did have time to myself, which was the only good thing now – since I wasn't as busy – I would watch television. Sometimes when I'd flip through channels I would see some preacher casting – or think he was – a demon out of some poor individual. But what really got me was when I would come across something on the news about some poor Muslim woman being stoned to death for some really stupid reason, like showing her skin!

I wanted to puke!

Who was this God anyway? He certainly wasn't a loving one!

Therefore, something inside me told me that it wasn't a god at all that made these laws – it was man!

No loving, caring, decent God would treat women like they were second-class citizens, let them be treated by men's double standards, let them be treated like nothing more than either sex objects or slaves.

I wanted to follow in my mother's footsteps and just run away. But where would I go? I didn't attend college like she had begged me to. And when I did try, Greg wouldn't let me. I was stuck just like my poor mother. But somehow she had managed to save up enough money to get away. I couldn't help but wonder how she had done it.

One night while I lay in bed unable to sleep, listening to the howling wind that had blown up a storm, I remembered the dream I had had of the gorgeous blond man. But why I thought of him at that moment? I had no idea. He had said he would be watching me. If he was real, was he still watching? Did he know of the hell I had been going through? If so, did he care? And if he cared, why hadn't he helped me?

I lay awake until the birds began singing a little after four a.m. I was tired, but knew I wasn't going to get any sleep, so I got up and took a shower. Greg was still asleep when I came out. Lucky bastard! I thought. I had such mixed feelings for him and my dad anymore. I really wasn't sure if I would continue to love them or not.

I made a fresh pot of coffee and went out to sit on the top porch step. The first rays of sunlight were stretching up over the horizon. It wasn't exactly cool, simply pleasant, but would be heating up soon. Though it wasn't often that I was up this early, I did love the fresh air this time of morning.

Cattycornered across the street to our right was our neighbor Jerry Crown, a family lawyer. He came out and, seeing me, smiled gregariously and waved. He was always friendly. I waved back. He didn't say anything though, just jumped in his BMW, backed out of the concrete driveway, waved again and took off to the right. He always left early; told me once that he went to the gym every morning before going on into the office.

Jerry and his wife Charlotte, a gorgeous bleached blonde, came to our church once in a while – Probably because it was convenient. Jerry even stated once that he didn't adhere to any particular denomination, but he believed in God. They mostly came on the holidays like Easter and Christmas and occasionally graced us with their presence otherwise.

I knew they weren't real religious, though, and not because they didn't come to church regularly. For one, Charlotte was a carefree soul. She always seemed really, really happy; nearly always smiling and in a good mood. Yelling, "Hey there, sugar!" when she'd see me.

I can honestly say that though I didn't know her well, I believe I liked her about as much as I liked anyone. At least, I always felt I didn't have to put on the false face and sweet air expected of me by my father, husband and regular parishioners.

I wondered if she realized just how lucky she was. Oh how I envied her freedom!

She dressed the way she wanted, oftentimes in attire that would have brought forth wrath from my dad and husband, had I adorned myself with such clothing. Nevertheless, I couldn't help but notice that neither of my two pastors ever made any comments to Charlotte or her husband about the way she dressed.

On the contrary, I caught not only Greg, but my father, looking at her in ways that suggested they weren't entirely cordial.

In spite of their strict, rigid teachings and limitations on me, they were definitely men. It was all too clear that they liked Charlotte's almost see-through blouses, tight jeans, short skirts, heavy makeup, and enticing perfumes.

That old double standard!

I was really beginning to hate men – Christian men, anyway. And I suppose I should add Jewish and Muslim as well.

The door opened then and Greg came up behind me. "What are you doing up so early? And why are you sitting out here?"

I stood, turned, faced him and said, "Wishing I was Charlotte." And I walked past him.

He grabbed my arm to stop me. "Why would you want to be like her, Brenda? She's married, but still dresses like a trollop."

With a contemptuous laugh, I replied, "So! Have you told Jerry that you basically think his wife is a whore?" I yanked my arm back and went on in the house.

Now pissed, he came in behind me and slammed the door. "Stop, Brenda!"

I turned and eyed him straight on. "What? You going to hit me now?"

His brow wrinkled in a dark frown. "What is wrong with you?"

"Don't tell me you don't know. You basically called Jerry's wife a whore just because she's a free woman and her husband doesn't mind her looking her best, but I've seen you *and* Dad drooling over her when you thought no one else was looking. Hypocrites!" I went on to the bathroom, shut the door and locked it. I didn't want to talk to him anymore. I just wanted to be left alone.

He came to the door and stood behind it. "We're not finished, Brenda!"

"Oh yes we are! If you want me to make your breakfast, drop it right now! I need time to cool down. Or you can cook your own breakfast."

Silence for a long moment, but then I heard his footsteps fading down the hall. Apparently he didn't want to go without his breakfast. "Jerk!"

*

I hadn't seen Nancy since that awful night when Dad and Greg dragged me before the entire church and everything had turned into a virtual nightmare. I was sure she was angry with me and probably didn't want any more to do with me. Still, I wondered how she was and what she was doing. What's more, I wanted to ask her about the dark clouds that had attacked everyone. I also had been craving coffee ice cream for some time, and I considered Baskin Robbins' the best. I had been fighting the urge for several days, but I finally gave in one especially hot afternoon when I was out and about on church errands.

When I walked in, they were busy. Nancy and a young Asian man were the only two working. Nancy saw me, but didn't say anything. The young man finished with his customer first and asked if he could help me. I went to order, but Nancy suddenly spoke up and said she wanted to talk to me, for them to switch customers. He shrugged and said it didn't matter to him and she came on over, and in a low voice asked, "You okay?"

I was surprised. I had expected anger, not concern. "Not really," I honestly replied.

Nodding for me to come around to the side so we could talk, I followed, not sure what she was going to say.

"I am so sorry that Aunt Ruth got you in trouble!"

"I… I thought you were angry with me?"

She shook her head no. "Why would I be angry with you?"

"I thought you considered me a traitor or something."

"No! No! No!" She glanced over at the Asian boy. "You okay, Mike?"

"I'm okay. I've got everyone covered."

She glanced at the clock on the back wall. Still speaking to Mike, she said, "It's three. I'm going to take a five minute break now."

"Ok," he replied, flashing a white-toothed smile. "Then I get mine."

"Naturally," she said, grinning. She turned to me. "Mike's a saint." She thought about it a second. "Well… not actually. But you get my drift. He's great."

"There's something I have to ask you about, Nancy."

She focused on my face. "Toss it at me. What is it?"

"That night… when Greg and my dad dragged me into the church… Well, they were… well… pretty much trying to exorcise a demon out of me."

"I heard." Her brown eyes flashed angrily. "I was really pissed when my aunt told me what she did. Honestly, I'm done with her now. I have put up with her crap for a couple of years. Went to church with her to try and appease her. Wasn't enough. She had to betray you. She had to betray me. I don't care if she is the only aunt I have. I have had it!"

"Seriously?"

"Damn right. Seriously!"

"I was so afraid you were mad at me."

"Why on Earth would I be mad at you? You're the one who was railroaded into confessing something you shouldn't have had to confess. I know. Aunt Ruth told me all about it." She grinned smugly then. "Right before I kicked her fat derriere out of my apartment and told her I didn't want to ever see her ugly face again."

"Oh! Did she tell you about the little dark clouds attacking us?"

"Yep."

"Did she tell you that they left when I asked Jesus for forgiveness?"

"Yep!"

"What were they?"

"I'm not sure, Brenda… Astral entities of some kind. I have seen them before, and they have never harmed me or anyone of my pagan friends. I don't think they were there to harm you. Did any of them attack you, specifically?"

I had to think about it a minute. "Actually, no. I was so terrified I freaked out, not knowing what was going on. I just did what I thought I should under the circumstances. Reacted in a way I was brought up to react. I called on Jesus for forgiveness. They didn't leave immediately. It took a few minutes. They still attacked some of the parishioners, but eventually left. So, I figured that I had been in the wrong after all. But it sure as hell didn't feel like it."

"Yeah. That comes from that Christian brainwashing. I am so glad my folks didn't raise me up in the church. Actually, my dad was an atheist. And mom just didn't care. She said she believed in something. Believed there was a God, but she didn't believe in all the religious mumbo-jumbo her sister believed in."

"You're lucky."

"Tell me about it." She glanced back over her shoulder to check the clock and then turned back to me. "Hey. If you can get away, come by one of these evenings."

"Are you kidding? I'm a prisoner in my own home. I had errands to run. Otherwise, I wouldn't have gotten by here to see you."

"That is no way to live, Brenda. You need to get away from there!"

I bobbed my head yes. "That's an understatement. But I don't have my own money. I don't have a job. Neither Dad nor Greg will let me get a job. They say my duties for the church are my job, even though I don't really have more than a few dollars at a time to spend for myself."

"I am so sorry. And I hate to say it, so glad I'm not in your shoes. Wicca is awesome. You would have been happy with us."

"Maybe. But that's out of the question now."

She touched the top of my hand with her fingertips. "If you really want to find a way, you will. You know there's that old saying: "Where there's a will there's a way."

"I hope you're right." I realized I'd been there a little too long. "Well, I'd better get. And thanks so much for not being angry with me."

"Never! It's that traitor aunt of mine that I am pissed at. Not you. You come back to see me anytime you can. Now, you wanted a coffee cone. Right?"

I nodded yes.

"Two scoops?"

"Always."

She got my ice-cream and handed it over the counter to me. "And no charge."

"You're sure?"

"Absolutely! I'm assistant manager now. Got promoted a couple of weeks ago."

"Congratulations!"

"Thanks! I'm happy about it."

I thanked her again for the cone, said goodbye to her and Mike and left. I was now worried that I had been gone too long and couldn't get home fast enough.

Sure enough, Greg met me at the door, face drawn, angry. "Where you been?"

"I'm not a child! And this is a free country. I was running errands for *yours and Dad's church!* You're the one who sent me, remember?"

His brown narrowed. "What do you mean by 'yours and Dad's church'?"

"It's certainly not mine! Honestly, I hate church anymore! Hate it!" And I stormed off to the bathroom and locked the door behind me, so he couldn't follow. I shook uncontrollably. I had to wonder: Had I reacted too fast when I had given in that night at the church? Had I betrayed myself? "Shit!" I hissed. "Shit! Shit! Shit!"

"Brenda! Open the door!"

"Not until you promise to leave me alone!"

"You've been talking to that witch, Nancy, haven't you?"

I didn't answer.

"You had an ice cream cone in your hand when you came in – Baskin Robbins. I know that's where she works."

"As I said before, *Greg*, it's a free country!"

"You are in danger of losing your soul! Don't you care?"

"It can't be any worse than living in the prison I'm living in now!" I retorted.

I heard him gasp and quickly leave. I knew he was going over to the church after Dad. I opened the bathroom door and ran out the front, not bothering to take the car. I headed straight for the park, tossing what little was left of my cone in a park trash can soon as I arrived. There was a water fountain. I went straight to it and rinsed off my hands and face. Then I saw the bench where I had talked to the blond-headed man, Erick, that day and went straight for it. I saw Dad's car pass by, Greg in the passenger seat. I could see them, but they couldn't see me. I figured it was only a matter of time before they realized I might be at the park. So I jumped up and headed for the opposite side, behind the restroom building out of sight, hoping they wouldn't think to search for me there.

This time I plopped down in front of a tall tree and leaned my back against it. I closed my eyes and did my best to slow down my breathing, for I had been panting from running so fast and so hard. I wondered if Erick was around. I know I hadn't seen any signs of him upon entering the park. I opened my eyes, leaned forward and looked around in all directions. Only I couldn't see through the bathroom building. I saw no one that even vaguely resembled him. "Dammit!"

I leaned my head back again and tried to clear my mind of all thoughts and anguish, for utterly devastated was the only thing I was capable of feeling, and that I didn't want to feel at all.

I'm not sure how long I sat there, and I must have drifted off to sleep, for suddenly a loud, familiar voice said, "Here she is!"

My eyes popped open to see my father standing there glaring down at me while mopping his brow with a white handkerchief. Greg caught up with him right then.

"I just want to be left alone," I said.

"There's something seriously wrong with you, young lady!" my dad stated angrily.

"And there's seriously something wrong with *you*! You can't see what you are doing to me? You can't see what you did to Mom! You take no blame for any of it." I turned my attention to Greg. "And you're just as bad, Greg! You've become my father's clone!"

"What are you talking about, Brenda? I've tried to be understanding. I have."

"Maybe a little. At first. But you are so freakin' wrapped up in the church and what Dad wants you to do, that you can't see the forest for the trees."

"I'm doing God's work, Brenda."

"Yeah… Sure you are! Just keep telling yourself that," was my sarcastic response.

"You need to come home. Now!" Dad ordered.

"I am not a thirteen-year-old runaway! I am a grown woman! You expect me to carry the load of three people! And it wouldn't be so bad, if you actually cared about what my needs might be. But you don't. Everything has to be what you dictate as God's will. Well, I've got a newsflash for you. You've set yourself up on some pedestal, thinking you have all the answers, when you don't. You're doing what *you* want to do. No God is making you do it!"

Dad suddenly slapped me hard across the face. "I will not take your insolence!"

Even Greg appeared shocked. He just stared at Dad in disbelief.

My face hurt. It hurt like hell. But I wasn't going to back down to him. Not this time.

"Go to hell!" I screamed.

He raised his hand to hit me again, but Greg intercepted his wrist. "No! No, Dad! That's not the way. We don't beat our women into obedience."

Dad suddenly got this really weird look in his eyes and he slowly turned to Greg. He just stood there for a minute, pondering. After a bit, he said, "I'm sorry. I guess I lost it there for a minute."

"I'm not the one you should apologize to," Greg replied.

I was almost as stunned by Greg standing up for me as I was by my Dad hitting me.

Dad turned to me. "I'm *sorry*, Brenda. I just want you to come home."

"Not if you're going to yell at me and treat me like I'm some lowlife."

He lowered his head, looking down at the ground. "I won't. I promise. Just come home... Please?"

Dubiously, I looked at Greg.

He nodded yes.

"Okay."

Greg took my hand and assisted me in standing. He held his arm around me while we walked back to the car. I wasn't sure where any of this was going, but I knew that for the moment, my husband was at my side.

A male jogger with shoulder-length blond hair pulled back in a ponytail was coming down the path just as we approached the street and car. I recognized him instantly – Erick! And right as he passed by in front of us, I could have sworn he winked my way. After he passed, we continued on to the car. I couldn't help wondering, though, if Erick had somehow had an influence on the outcome of what had just transpired. Then again, maybe I was just plain nuts. My father and husband had finally succeeded in driving me completely insane.

Chapter Five

Things really weren't a lot better, not where my dad was concerned anyway. Still, the fact that Greg stood up for me that day meant a lot to me. Also, he was trying hard to be a better husband; actually began to cut his time with Dad down and spend more time with me at our place.

He even served me breakfast in bed one Saturday. Not only was I surprised by the gesture, I was equally amazed by the fact that he could cook. He made me the best scrambled eggs I'd ever had, cinnamon toast, bacon and freshly, hand-squeezed orange juice.

"That was delicious!" I said when he came in to get my tray. "I had no idea you could cook."

His smile held a hint of pride. "I used to think I would be a chef when I grew up," he explained. "Used to cook for my mom and dad. That is, before we moved here and I began frequenting your church."

"What changed your mind?"

"I felt the call to the Lord, Brenda."

"Yeah. I should have known better than to ask that question."

There was a flicker of hurt in his eyes. "You're still very angry with us, aren't you?"

"I'd be lying if I said I wasn't. But, I can see you are really trying. You're trying harder than I ever thought you would." I threw back my covers, got up and began making the bed. Greg set the tray aside and helped me. I smiled thankfully. "You do love me, don't you?"

"Yes I do, Brenda. And I am *so* sorry for the way we have treated you. Especially my part in all of it. That day in the park when Dad hit you – Well, it was a big eye-opener for me. It was for him too. Only, not as much." He looked away as though pained by what he believed.

"Greg, look at me. Please!"

He faced me again.

"I do love you. Honestly, I'm not sure I love you as much as I once did. Still, I do care for you deeply. And the change I've seen in you since that day in the park has brought us much closer." I smiled encouragingly. "I think that maybe there's a chance for us after all."

His eyes filled with tears. "Oh Brenda!" He grabbed me in his arms and hugged me tight. I could feel him shaking against me.

"It's okay, Greg. It's okay. I know you love me now. And I promise I will work with you. Work on our marriage."

He pulled back sniffling. I grabbed him a tissue from a box on the nightstand and handed it over. He honked into it and tossed it in the small trashcan by the bed. "And I will too. Dad may not like it, but from here on out, you come first."

"Seriously?" I could hardly believe my ears.

"Of course I will still assist in pastoring, etc. But you are the most important person in the world to me. I don't want to lose you – ever! From now on, if I have to choose between you and the church, I will choose you!"

"Oh my gosh!" I was crying too. "I would have never thought that I would hear you say something like that."

"Honestly, neither did I. But I got to thinking about our wedding vows and Matthew nineteen: six: Where it says 'let no may put asunder'—Well, I'm a man … Your husband. And your dad's a man. And the both of us were putting yours and my marriage asunder." He sniffled. "And the irony of it is – We were doing it in the name of the Lord! There's just something wrong with that."

"Oh Greg! I do love you!" I kissed him sweetly. Right at that moment, my heart leapt with joy. I felt everything was going to be all right from there on out. And it was for a while, but only a short while.

All of a sudden there was a rise of so-called demonic possessions in several of the local churches. At first Dad was, or appeared to be, sensible about it and stated before the whole congregation that it was a good possibility that many, if not all, of the 'demonic possessions' were simply mentally ill folks who could use a good psychologist. To my knowledge, Dad had never cast out any demons before anyway. I almost think the idea of it kind of frightened him.

Then one of our own parishioners, Jennifer Wilkes, an attractive twenty-year-old daughter of one of the deacons, Harry Wilkes and Jean Wilkes, began acting strangely one Sunday night service. At prayer call, she suddenly ran up to the platform and, throwing herself prostrate across the floor, began screaming obscenities at my Dad and Greg.

Dad was so shocked that he just stood there staring in incredulity with his mouth open. Greg was also stunned, but only momentarily, before going over to the young woman, who then jumped up and scratched him across the cheek, bringing blood.

Of course I quickly got up and ran to my husband, but he was caught up in the moment, reacting, I suppose as a lot of pastors would, laying his hands on the woman's head, praying and ordering the demon to come out of her in the name of Jesus.

Getting over his shock, Dad joined in, praying along with him. Jennifer clawed and fought them furiously, but they didn't back down. Harry came up too and took hold of his daughter from behind and they wrestled her to the floor. (Months later it was learned that she had been watching the local news about the alleged demonic possessions on the news before attending services that night.)

Of course, the entire congregation caught the fever of the moment and moved forward, standing around the intense scene.

I simply stared. Something just didn't sit right with me about the whole thing. I wasn't buying it. I could only watch for so long, and turned and went to the house and got the First Aid kit and brought it back to dress Greg's wound. By that time the 'demon' had been exorcised from Jennifer, and she was being cared for by Dad and a number of the church members.

I went up to Greg, who had pulled away from the scene now, simply observing, and had him sit down on the other front pew, opposite where the circus that Jennifer had created was going on.

He shrugged as he spoke to me. "I've never seen that happen before," he admitted. "I've heard of it… but never witnessed a possession."

"Honestly, Greg. You know what I think?"

He turned his gaze up to me. "What?"

"I think she was acting."

His brow furrowed. "No! That was too crazy. I don't believe she was acting."

"Okay. Think about it though. There is kind of a possession-fever going through the community. And people have a way of running with things when they get excited."

"That's true. Still, I don't believe that's the case here."

"All right," I said with a smile. "You're the professional. Simply voicing my perception of the whole thing."

Returning my smile, he said, "And your viewpoint is appreciated. You know that."

He stood then, as Dad was approaching, looking all smug and self-important.

I excused myself and took my seat, waiting for Jennifer and her family to exit the church, along with about half the congregation. It appeared that this one particular service was going to see an early finish.

I sat there for several minutes, while Dad and Greg discussed the events with the members who had remained. Tired of waiting, I went on out. It was dark now as I headed across the way to our house. That was when I saw Erick. He stood on the corner of our lot, under the streetlight. This time, he wore jeans and a red tee-shirt, and his golden hair hung gently at his shoulders. I glanced behind me and saw no one else coming out of the church, so I turned back and walked on up to him.

He flashed a beautiful smile of perfect teeth. "Interesting evening?"

"To say the least. More like a three-ring circus."

He chuckled, apparently amused. "You could say that."

"Were you there?"

"Witnessed the whole thing."

"Maybe I'm wrong, but I think she just wanted attention."

"Looks like she got it."

"Brenda!" Greg called from behind.

"Looks like your hubby wants you."

"Kind of looks that way."

"Well, you have a good rest of the evening."

"You too." I turned and waited for Greg to approach.

"Why didn't you wait for me?" he inquired.

"Just tired."

"What were you doing standing under the streetlight?"

"Talking to the tall blond-headed man that comes sometimes. Said his name is Erick."

"Huh? What blond-headed man? I didn't see anyone with you." Looking uncertain, he glanced around. "I don't see anyone around, Brenda."

I took a quick glance too. Erick was nowhere to be seen. "He's a jogger," I replied, returning my attention back to my husband. "Probably ran off before you got close enough to see him." I did wonder, though. That wasn't the first time Erick had just vanished on me. "Is everything squared away at the church? Or do you need me to go back and help with anything?"

"Your dad said it could wait until morning. I think this evening's service kind of shook him up. Truthfully, it rather unnerved me as well."

"I already voiced my opinion on the matter."

He went to protest but stopped himself. "Okay. Let's just go home and go to bed."

"Agreed."

That wasn't the end of it though. The fever had set in. It was as though the entire community had gone nuts with a rash of 'demonic possessions'. At the very next Wednesday prayer-meeting, Agnes Grafity, an elderly lady in her late sixties, who normally seemed mild-mannered, stood up suddenly in the middle of a prayer and screamed at Dad to go fuck himself.

I have to admit, that though embarrassing, I sniggered. I'm not sure why, but it struck me as comical. This time, Dad and Greg were prepared, had their scriptures picked out and ready for such an outburst. Dad and Greg, along with a couple of deacons, immediately had the elderly woman surrounded.

I have to hand it to her. I believe Agnes gave a better performance than Jennifer.

They got the old lady down on the floor, but she was still shrieking obscenities at the top of her lungs.

Greg held a wooden cross over Agnes' face and she spit on it, and called him a mother-fucker.

Suddenly, church service had become interesting.

I did, however, almost feel sorry for Greg. He really and truly believed the old woman was possessed. And I suppose Dad did too. Still, I harbored a lot of resentment towards him, and just could not bring myself to feel any pity for him. What's more, I was beginning to see that this was actually feeding his ego from the 'importance' of what he was doing.

Oh my God! I thought, and turned to glance at the church entrance. Erick stood just inside the door. He winked, shook his head at the transpiring spectacle, turned and walked out.

It was another ten minutes before the 'demon' was finally cast out. At which time, Agnes suddenly came to her senses and declared that she couldn't remember a thing.

I had my doubts. Seemed like a way of getting attention to me, albeit a bizarre way.

That wasn't the end.

The news media became involved. Not only the local newspapers but KWEX and WOAI were suddenly interested. Our community, including our church, even made the national news one Friday evening. I simply wanted to bury my head in a sand dune someplace, and didn't hesitate to hide at the first sign of reporters.

Of course, our church wasn't the only one caught up in the fever, but I know Dad soaked up the attention, and most of it did seem to be focused on us.

What really worried me though was Greg was beginning to see himself in a more important light. It was one thing dealing with my normally egotistical father, but Greg and I had finally been getting along for the first time in a while. Now this! I sensed I was losing my husband again. And I wasn't sure that I would get him back this time.

He and Dad threw some classes together on casting out demons – as though they had been doing it all their lives. I did try to talk some reason into Greg one evening while I had him captured long enough to sit down to a pot roast dinner. I noticed he was agitated but I thought it was because of all the hectic things going on. I suggested that they possibly were taking things too far, meaning that maybe they had taken on more than they could handle. He became pissed and haughtily told me I didn't know what I was talking about. It was at that time he reached in his back pocket and pulled out the folded paper of the witch's calendar that I had hidden in the church piano. "The piano tuner gave me this about an hour ago!" His eyes were now red with fury. "I know you put it there!"

"Months ago! I had forgotten all about it. I swear, Greg! I knew you'd be angry if you found it. I didn't know where else to hide it. But that was before! I'm not with the group now. Believe me!"

"Well! That's all nice and great," he sputtered sarcastically. "But I am pretty sure now that your dabbling in witchcraft could very well be responsible for all these demonic possessions, especially in our church! For all I know, that piece of paper has a curse on it, and that is why you left it in the piano."

That did it. Something inside me froze. I stood and glared at him, shaking so hard I was temporarily speechless.

"Sit down, Brenda! We're not finished! I didn't tell your father about this, but I should."

I found my voice and replied, "I really don't give a damn now if you do!" It was as if he had wrapped ice around my heart. At that moment, all the love and warmth I had felt for him, after our renewed feelings for one another, simply withered away and died – an autumn leaf blown away by the harsh winter wind. "Okay," I calmly replied, fully aware that I would not address it again.

There was no reason to.

I didn't sit, though. I just applied my anger into furiously cleaning up the mess in the kitchen, slamming pots and pans around and being as noisy as possible. I had no appetite. I just wanted him to eat his supper and go back to the church where Dad was waiting for him.

He did eat, though I had halfway expected him not to. Ignoring my fury in silence, he stuffed his face and pushed his plate aside. When he rose from his seat, he looked at me, tossed his napkin aside, and said, "Good roast." I had the distinct feeling that part of him wanted to say he was sorry, but he chose not to. It was too late anyway. I think he knew that. He hurried out the front door over to the church.

"Thanks!" I said to the empty room.

I knew Greg and Dad would probably stay up until midnight or later, plotting their tactics for fighting off all the 'demons'.

As far as I was concerned, the only demons around were the ones in their pinpointed heads.

"Idiots!" I spewed and went to the bedroom and plopped heavily down on the end of the bed. I wanted to leave. This time, for good. I wished that I knew where Mom was, but I didn't. That was when I once more wondered where she had acquired the money to leave Dad. Then it hit me. There was the grocery allowance for the church dinners and etc. She must have saved a portion of it every month until she had enough to get a place, just taking a little out at a time. But I didn't want to wait for three or four months. I was done.

I knew Dad kept it in a small safe in the church office. And I knew the combination; had known it since I was six. I couldn't get it at that time, for they were there. I would have to wait. Still, I wanted to get out of there as soon as I possibly could, so I pulled down one of the two large maroon duffle bags that Greg and I used when we traveled, which was rarely. Mine had my name on the side.

I quickly grabbed all my clean underwear out of the middle drawer of the chest – glad I had washed clothes earlier that day – and packed in three pairs of jeans, two sweat shirts, two blouses, and four colored tee-shirts, including my favorite yellow one with Tweetie Bird on the front.

I stuffed in two skirts and two dresses, threw in my brush, comb, hair spray, and a couple of sweaters, along with my black dress-pumps wrapped in a small grocery bag. It was all I could do to zip the duffle bag closed. I grabbed my toothbrush out of the bathroom and the partly used tube of Colgate – there was a brand new one that hadn't been opened. I left that for Greg. I dropped them in the side zip-pocket, closed it and went to the door. I looked across the way over to the church. Not seeing anyone, I figured I had a clear path. I had my keys in my pocket. I opened up the trunk of my car and tossed the bag in and closed it.

I went back in the house. I couldn't leave yet. I still had to get the money out of the church safe. I went ahead and took my shower, dressed for bed, but left out a clean change of clothes folded in the washroom. Greg rarely went in there, and I figured that he definitely wouldn't go in there at night. He'd be too tired when he and Dad finished up at the church. And even if he did, he probably wouldn't think anything about the folded clothes sitting on the dryer. Just believe I hadn't put them away yet.

After I showered and dressed for bed, I stuck the car keys in the toes of my tennis shoes. Except for the money, I was ready.

Greg finally came to bed just a little before one a.m. It wasn't five minutes before he was snoring. This was my chance. I eased out of bed, stopping only briefly at the door, listening. He was still snoring. I grabbed my clothes out of the washroom, dressed in the bathroom, but didn't bother to put on any makeup. I would do that later at a motel or wherever I ended up at.

Dressed, I headed over to the church, letting myself in the back door as the office was there. I knew the combination by heart. I am sure Dad would have never believed I would actually take money from the church. And there was a time when I wouldn't have even considered it. But due to things being the way they were, I figured I had no choice. I spun the dial on the safe to the right at 9 and then to the left at 6 and back at 3. It clicked, and I quickly opened it. There was at least a thousand dollars in twenties, and smaller bills. I counted out five hundred, not wanting to take it all, and stuffed it in my purse. I shut the safe and spun the dial and left out the back, locking up again. Then I ran back to the house where my Kia was parked, got in, started it up and went to pull out and then slammed on my brakes.

A patrol car pulled in the drive blocking my path. Headlights shone in my face, almost blinding me.

"Oh shit!"

Dad was suddenly there, greeting the two officers, one a young black male and the other was a white woman in her forties. The woman grabbed me and shoved me against the police car, cuffing my hands behind my back.

Dad stepped up to my left side, face contorted in anger and dismay. "It never would have occurred to me that it could be you! My own daughter! How could you do such a thing, Brenda?"

I didn't say anything. The female officer was spewing my Miranda rights to me.

Dad continued, "I was still in the church about ready to walk out the front when I heard someone enter into my office. I quickly called 911, but realized it was you when I saw you jump in your car."

Greg ran out the front door then, tucking in his shirt, looking shocked by what he saw. "I woke up to the lights flashing," he said. He addressed me, "What on earth has come over you?"

"If you don't know by now, you never will," I calmly replied.

The black officer, aware now that I was Dad's daughter, asked Dad if he was sure he wanted to press charges.

Dad looked at me long and hard and then replied, "Definitely! She's never going to learn if she doesn't pay for her sins."

"Okay," the cop said, and nodded for the female to put me in the back. I was shoved in and the door locked.

Greg just stood there staring and shaking his head. He really did not understand. I almost felt sorry for him, but not quite.

Dad, well, he definitely didn't have a clue. He never understood why Mom left, and he wasn't about to understand now why I was so desperate to leave that I was willing to steal money from the church.

Neither of them got it, and I knew they never would. Now I would have a police record. How high a price did I have to pay for my freedom? What Greg had said to me earlier had been the icing on the cake. Well, this was it all boxed up and ready to go. No matter what happened to me now, I knew I was done with the both of them for good.

My only regret was I had no idea where Mom was.

Chapter Six

Dad and Greg were at my hearing. One glance Greg's way told me that he wasn't as keen on going through with this as Dad. Dad was pissed though and wasn't about to back down.

When Judge Whitteker asked me as to why I stole from my own father and church, I told the truth – That living with such a controlling father and husband was pure hell and I would do anything short of murder to be free of them.

I could see by the look in the elderly judge's gray eyes after scanning my father's stern, cold face and my reluctant-to-comment husband that he felt kind of sorry for me. However, he had to abide by the law in passing sentence. At one point he did ask Dad if he was sure he wanted to follow through with the charges, and Dad didn't hesitate in replying that he did.

I had a court-appointed attorney, but when the petite Asian female by the name of Doris Lee asked me how I wanted to plea, I said that I was guilty.

I was sentenced to a month in the county jail. I know that the sentence could have been more severe, but it was more than apparent that Judge Whitteker didn't really feel I belonged there.

Although I knew that Greg wasn't as bent on punishing me as my father, he still didn't have the balls to stand up for me. So, when he tried to come visit me in jail, I refused to see him. As far as I was concerned, we were done.

Greg did have a letter delivered to me in jail. He said he loved me and that he was sorry for all that had happened; that he knew he was just as much to blame as anyone. He also hoped that I would come back to him after I was released from jail, but he did understand if I should choose not to. He also told me that the door would always be open, and if I chose not to stay with him, that I could pick up my things whenever I was released. I didn't bother to reply, but I felt a little better, knowing that I could get my things without an argument.

I felt that Greg did speak from the bottom of his heart, but I knew all too well from past experience that he could change and be good to me – for a while – and then he would, most likely, revert back to his old behavior, once he felt as though we were on solid ground again. I had been there and done that more than once, and it was one time too many for me. It was like the old saying, 'Trick me once, shame on you. Trick me twice, shame on me.'

I wasn't sure where I would go when I was released. There were numerous parishioners I could have stayed with had I not been labeled a common criminal, but I was sure no one would take me in now; positive Dad had made me out to be the worst of sinners.

The only person I felt I might confide in was Nancy. I hoped, oh how I hoped, she was still working for Baskin Robbins and knew of some place I could stay, and where I might possibly find a job.

Of course, there was Erick, but I wasn't entirely sure just who he was. What's more, I had no clue how to get in touch with him, other than maybe hanging out around the park. There were no guarantees with that scenario either. Just because he had been good to me in the past, didn't mean he would take me in.

The day I was released, I went straight to Baskin Robbins only to learn that Nancy had moved away. I also quickly learned that the middle-aged Hispanic woman I spoke with had taken Nancy's place. There were no more openings. Discouraged, I slowly walked to my car. At least, I still had that. Problem was, I had no money, and when the half tank of gas ran out, I wouldn't be able to buy anymore. So, not knowing what else to do, I drove to the park that I had run to before. There were a couple of parking areas. I could, at least, park my car there during the day. I wasn't sure if I could stay there at night, though.

I almost wished I could go back to jail. There, I had a roof over my head and regular meals, even though they weren't always that good. Still, it beat going hungry.

I had been apprehensive to return to the house in spite of Greg's making it clear that I was welcome. I still felt uneasy about seeing him. Most of all, I did not want to see my father. By now, I truly despised him. In fact, I was pretty sure that I had no love for him at all anymore. He had, quite successfully, killed it.

I did have my iPhone that Greg had been nice enough to keep the bill paid – which I fully intended to reimburse him for – and a car charger. It was something to do. I went online and began searching the web. I came across the Joy of Satan website. It had been elaborately done and caught my eye right away. The inverted pentacle in red sparkled and turned as though it were a chime in the wind. I'm not exactly sure why I remained there for any length of time, considering my strict Christian upbringing. But then, maybe that was the very reason I was compelled to continue.

Nothing else had worked for me in any positive way.

Not Christianity and certainly not Wicca! That had backfired big time!

I'm not certain what really came over me at that moment: defiance, anger, hatred, and complete loss of faith, whatever. Then maybe it was all those things combined? I feverishly began reading all the testimonials on how dedicating to Satan had changed lives for the better. I couldn't believe it! How could dedicating to Satan possibly make one's life better? The thought of dedicating to such a powerful being that I had been brought up to believe was the very epitome of evil simply terrified me.

Still, compelled, I read on.

What this website was saying was that the stories of the Bible had things all twisted around – that Satan was actually the good God! What? I realized I was shaking, I was so unglued. How was this possible?

There was something about the tree of knowledge actually being a metaphor for the Kundalini Serpent. What, I asked myself, is the Kundalini Serpent? I read on to see that it is this part of creation, of our true spirituality, that lives inside all of us. And if one opens themselves up enough that the serpent will rise and we will suddenly awaken to the true realities of the universe and creation. That, in essence, we all had to potential to reach godhood!

What's more, Satan not only wanted, but still wants, this for all of us.

The other religions of the world had been keeping this knowledge from mankind for thousands of years. Why?

To control the masses out of fear!

My first reaction to all this *was* fear. I got off the website and sat there trembling. I couldn't believe that I had let myself read that much.

What was wrong with me?

I'm not sure how long I sat there, doing my best to process all that I had read, and that was only the beginning. There was much more information on that website; something about Ea (pronounced Arya) being Satan's real name.

I suddenly had the urge to pee really badly. I stuck my phone in the hip pocket of my jeans and got out of my car, locking it, and headed for the brick building about half a block to my left where the bathrooms were. It was pretty dark inside, in spite of the many lamps situated around the park. There weren't any inside. I did manage to relieve myself though, and then promptly washed my hands and dried them the best I could with one of those blow driers. I always hated those things. Paper towels worked far better. But I could see where it might be more economical money-wise and tidy-wise to not have a bunch of paper around.

I stepped just out the door, and someone to my right said hello. I snapped my head around. "Erick!"

Again in jogging attire and his hair in a ponytail, he smiled warmly from where he stood, leaning with his back against the building. He'd been waiting for me! "Kind of late for a young woman to be alone in the park," he said, eyebrow hiked questioningly.

"I have no place else to go," I honestly replied.

"There are shelters. But I admit that they aren't necessarily the best places to stay."

"I know. I've seen them when doing charity work for the church."

He sniggered slightly as though he found something funny.

"What?"

"Not laughing at you, Brenda. Just at the irony of it all."

"Irony of what?"

"The world. The corruptness. One: churches supposedly helping the needy and homeless but only if they will come to their church. Two: Once they get the poor souls there, they call them sinners and make them feel even worse about themselves than they already do. But, if they will confess their 'sins' to the Lord, etc...etc... then they will be forgiven! But they have to live a life of self-denial."

I was astounded by Erick's words. And I wondered at the timing. Did he know what I had been doing before I went to the bathroom?

He turned his bright blue eyes – and yes, they were very bright for it to be night – to me and said, "It's all a big joke, you know?"

"Ah... I' not sure what you mean?"

"Think about it. Sex is frowned upon and promoted as evil. Yet, without sex mankind wouldn't be here. And not only mankind, but the rest of life! Sex is the generative, creative power of existence! There is absolutely nothing wrong with sex! The true evil is the ugly, twisted and perverted ideas driven into the minds of unknowing souls."

I think my jaw dropped about a foot.

He grinned at my reaction but continued. "There's that double standard that I'm sure you are all too aware of. It's okay for a man to look but not for the woman, so forth and so on. A man can have an affair and it pretty much be overlooked, but not a woman. And the Christian church is not the worst. Just look at the news. There are other religions far worse."

I hadn't been paying too much attention to the news lately, but I had heard about all the warfare going on overseas. I nodded yes.

"You know, stifling the natural urge for sex is not only harmful for your body, it stops your spirit from growing."

Remembering what I had read about the Kundalini, my eyes widened at that. "Say what?"

Again, he apparently found my astonishment somewhat amusing. He laid a gentle hand on my shoulder. "You're tired. Why don't I walk you back to your car? If you want, I can stay with you until morning?"

I wasn't sure how to react to his offer.

"Don't worry, Brenda. You will be more than safe with me. I will sit in the back seat while you get some z's. How does that sound?"

For some reason I knew I could trust him. I nodded yes. "That would be awesome. Thanks!"

He laid an arm around my shoulder and escorted me back to my car. There he slipped into the backseat, and I slid in the front. I turned and looked at him. "You sure you'll be okay back there? You're kind of tall, and this is a Kia Rio, not one of the bigger cars."

"I'll be fine. You just get some rest." He winked at me then and stretched out the best he could with his long legs and leaned his head back and closed his eyes.

"Okay... Night."

"Night," he responded without opening his eyes.

I woke up right before dawn and he was still there, apparently sleeping. At least, he appeared to be. So I fell back to sleep. When morning came and the sun was out bright I woke up again to find him gone.

"Okay," I said to myself. "I never even heard the door open."

I sat there briefly, trying to get my bearings. I needed to pee again. So I got out and made it to the bathroom and back. I desperately needed to bathe and change clothes. I decided that maybe I could find a restroom at a service station and sponge bathe there. I didn't trust cleaning up in the park bathroom, as there were no closed doors on the outside. Just short brick walls that turned the corner until you entered the bathroom. Doors on the stalls, but that was all.

I slid back into my car and started the ignition. That was when I was startled by a knuckle knocking on my window – Greg! I shook my head no. I didn't want to talk to him.

"Please! Just hear me out," he begged.

I rolled down the window. "I'm not coming back to you, Greg. Don't even try to talk me into it."

He looked hurt, but didn't let that deter him. "That's not why I'm here, Brenda. I wasn't able to sleep at all last night, wondering where you were and if you were okay."

"Really?" I said flatly, not sure I believed him.

"I had a feeling you might be here at the park. So I decided to come look. And here you are."

"And I'm about to leave."

"Please! Just let me finish?"

I exhaled with frustration but said okay.

"I am not asking you to come back to me. And I know you don't want to be my wife anymore. But, as someone who does care about your wellbeing, I can't just sit back and wonder if you are in an alley somewhere… possibly hurt… or worse… dead."

"What are you getting at, Greg?"

"I told you before that the door is open to you."

I shook my head adamantly. "I appreciate that, but I'm not coming back!"

"Not asking you to come back to me. Just asking you to take advantage of my offer of a place for you to stay until you get a job and can get your own place."

"I'm not sure I'm comfortable with that."

"I promise not to try and get you back! Just be free to bathe, fix yourself meals, etc. Don't even worry about cooking for me. And you can stay as long as it takes for you to get on your feet. Promise! No strings attached!"

I could see in his eyes that he was sincere. He meant it. "But you can't stop Dad from trying… Greg, I won't put up with Dad."

"I talked to him already. Told him I wanted you to have a safe haven, and without our bothering you. I admit, it took some doing, but he finally agreed."

I blew out air and looked off at some crows in the tops of a tall tree. I did want a decent bath something awful. I turned back to his hopeful face. It would make him feel better if I agreed. And I realized that part of it was his being able to live with himself. As a devout Christian he couldn't justify himself in knowing he didn't try everything he could to keep his wife safe. "Okay," I finally said. "But only until I get a job and my own place."

He closed his eyes in gratitude. "Thank you, Jesus!"

"I'll be over that way in a few minutes."

Eyes open again, he smiled with great relief. "Okay. See you then."

Truth was, I wanted to drive around the park and see if I could spot Erick anywhere, even though he'd probably gone on home. Wherever that was? I didn't see him, of course, so I drove on to the house.

Greg was standing outside Dad's house talking to him in what I could see was kind of a heated argument, but he smiled and waved for me to pull on in, so I did. I wasted not a second in getting out of the car and letting myself inside. Fresh coffee was made. I rushed over and helped myself to a cup. A caffeine fix was something I really needed at that moment.

Greg came in then smiling marginally, but I could see things weren't just right.

"Dad's not happy, is he?"

"Not really. But he's agreed to keep his promise." He helped himself to coffee and joined me at the table. "There are eggs and bacon, if you want to cook yourself breakfast? I already ate."

"Maybe in a little bit, Greg. I just want to sit here and savor this coffee and then I'm going to take a long hot shower."

He sat there for another minute or two and finished off his coffee. I know he wanted to say more, but also understood that there wasn't anything that was going to change my mind. He stood and gently laid his hand on my shoulder. "Gonna go discuss Sunday morning's sermon with your father. Just make yourself at home. You know where everything is."

"I do. Thank you, Greg!" I said, allowing myself to smile.

That seemed to make him happy. "You're welcome." He left and headed across the way to the church.

*

Greg kept his word. He didn't bother me at all other than mostly to say good morning or goodnight, just simple and polite pleasantries. I slept on the sofa. He had offered me the bed, but I thought better of it. To me, that was like inviting him to bed. After all, it was his house. What's more, I didn't want mixed messages.

Dad made no efforts to come to the house. Apparently Greg had made it very clear that he was to keep his distance from me. I could see it was stressful to Greg, but he said everything was okay. As long as he fulfilled his church duties, what he did at home was his business.

It was more than clear: Not only was I through with Dad, he was through with me. Sometimes I think he actually believed he was a chosen prophet of God. He was that cocky.

Greg could have easily gone that way, but I think that he truly did love me, and that alone had kept him from becoming the total insensitive jerk that Dad had become. For that, I was grateful. It was clear to me that Dad never really loved Mom. I am sure that was one of the things that had made it easier for her to leave. She knew it.

I finally got a job – at the library, which was only four blocks away, walking distance. I think Greg was relieved on one hand, and on the other, he knew that as soon as I saved enough money that I would be moving out. It was a good thing too, for I had long run out of money and didn't have enough for gas for my car. Greg, however, had lent me money for gas, enough for job-hunting. I promised to pay it back as soon as I received my first paycheck. He said it wasn't a problem. He knew I'd pay him back.

And I did.

One check wasn't enough to move out yet, but I figured I would have enough in about two months. So, I eagerly tucked my money in a new checking account for just myself. That way I knew it was safe and untouchable by my dad or my husband. At that point, I know Greg wouldn't have tried to take it anyway. Dad, on the other hand, might have come up with some self-righteous reason to try and bleed it out of me.

I was actually beginning to feel good about myself, for the first time in I couldn't remember when. In fact, I wasn't sure I had ever felt so good about myself, not in my entire life.

The reason being was I having a taste of freedom. I loved it!

There were busy days at the library and not so busy days. On the days when most of the books were put away and it was slow, I would find a book to browse through or surf the internet. Mrs. Peters, Miranda, the elderly head librarian, didn't care. She let me know more than once that she had always wanted a daughter. She'd had two sons, Rob and Michael, both married and living in Los Angeles. But I was like the daughter she never had.

There were a couple of other girls who worked there, Mae and Elsie, but they were kind of immature and were always talking about clothes, hanging out at the mall, and carousing, and didn't seem to think life was about anything else. They were the total opposite of me. Not that they were in the wrong, just very different. Miranda said I was refreshingly diverse, like the air on a spring morning. I told her she was sweet, and she gave me a motherly hug.

Of course, my being around Miranda made me miss my own mother. Where was she? Would I ever see or hear from her again? I was truly beginning to fear that I wouldn't.

Chapter Seven

One Friday night when I was working the late shift – the library was open until eleven during the week and midnight on the weekends – a rather handsome, dark-haired young man came in the library. He wore jeans and a black tee-shirt and a beautiful silver chain with a strange black stone that had a symbol that I had seen before but didn't have a clue as to what it stood for.

"Interesting necklace," I said, as I checked out his books on ancient history for him.

He brought his hooded brown eyes up to mine and said, "Thanks!"

I felt a sudden sense of power from him unlike nothing I'd ever felt from anyone before.

"Is it Masonic?" I inquired.

A slight, mysterious smile curved the edges of his mouth. "It's a sigil," he replied.

"Not Masonic?"

I had the distinct feeling he was inwardly amused by my questions. "No. Not Masonic."

"Does it mean anything in particular?"

"I just like it," he replied, grabbed up his books, turned and walked away.

It was time to close up, and with no one else in the library, I locked up and headed for home. Since it was late, and I had a few paychecks under my belt now, I had my car. I walked during the day when the sun was shining, but when it was night or raining I took my car.

That sigil stuck in my mind.

Greg was in bed and asleep when I reached the house. He kept his door closed when I worked late so my coming in wouldn't disturb him. I readied for bed: showered, brushed my teeth, donned my Hello Kitty pajamas that Greg had given me for Christmas, and decided to see if I could find that sigil on his laptop. He had left it on the kitchen table.

He didn't mind my using it, as long as I cleaned up my cookies and ran a quick virus scan before logging off. Immediately I looked up sigils. I found it pretty quick and just stared at it.

It was the sigil of Lucifer!

The mysterious man in the library was a Satanist!

Though a bit strange, he had seemed nice enough. But was he? At that time, I had some really bad hang-ups about Satanism. One doesn't get over years of intense conditioning easily.

I immediately cleaned up my search history, cookies and ran a quick scan and got off. I went to bed, but I didn't fall asleep right away. I just could not get that sigil out of my head. Nor could I forget the sense of power I had felt from the dark-haired man.

Not in all my life as a Christian had I felt that kind of power from anyone. There were a few pastors, clergy, that I had felt kind of an electrical zap from a time or two, like when one walks across a rug and touches someone else and gets shocked, but this man's energy was different. I could not deny that I had been in the presence of someone powerful.

And he was a Satanist!

Should I have been frightened of him?

I wasn't really sure.

I had not seen or heard from Erick in several days. I did think of him often, wondering where he was and exactly who he was. I still was pretty sure he wasn't exactly human, but then I had no one else to compare him too. I knew I would be eternally grateful for his caring and consideration of me. I just wondered if I would see him again.

According to Greg, Dad had really gotten into the laying of hands on the church members. And Greg was getting into it. I listened politely as he told me with much enthusiasm about how he and dad were casting out demons and more and more people were talking in tongues. I didn't say much, but I didn't argue with him either, and knowing Greg, he mistook it that I was interested. I didn't tell him otherwise.

So, one Sunday evening – there wasn't anything on television to take my interest – I decided to walk over to the church and slipped quietly in, the doors had been left wide open, since it was hot and Dad preferred it to running up the electric bill with air conditioning – and sat down on an empty back pew. All the members had gathered up to the front of the church, standing around Dad and Greg, as they went from member to member, laying their hands on them and praying. At which point, most of them would break out speaking in 'tongues'.

Sounded like gibberish to me.

One woman simply rambled, "La…La…La…La…La…La," over and over.

I couldn't help but notice the glow in Dad's face, and Greg was starting to become just as enthused.

Dad definitely thought he was a chosen disciple, and Greg was being infected by this insane charismatic fever.

Shit! I thought. That was when I realized someone had sat down to my right.

Erick!

Glad to see him, I smiled amiably.

He returned the smile and then nodded slightly, rolling his eyes towards the door, as though to ask me if I wanted to go outside.

My response was a yes nod.

He stood and went on out.

I followed.

We remained on the church porch for a moment. He stared up at the stars which were unusually vivid, even for being in the city limits, as there was no moon. "I love it when the stars are bright," he commented.

I agreed.

Gesturing with an outward held hand, he asked me if I wanted to take a stroll, and I said yes.

We headed in the direction of the park. I couldn't help but thinking how utterly handsome – not handsome – gorgeous he was.

He was the picture of perfection. Flawless. I couldn't help it, it just slipped out. "You're beautiful, you know that?"

He stopped walking, and I heard a faint chuckle. "Thank you."

Embarrassed, I apologized. "I shouldn't have said that."

"Why? I don't mind a compliment."

"One doesn't normally go around telling a man he's beautiful. But you are!" I know I blushed, and I was glad it was dark. This night he had on a white dress shirt and black pants; looked really, really nice. It was as though I couldn't feast my eyes on him enough. "What is it about you?" I asked.

"Want to clarify that question?"

"I think I may have brought this up before. At least, I thought it. You're not ..." I took a deep breath and exhaled. "I guess what I am trying to say is – You're no ordinary man, are you?"

Our eyes locked momentarily and the immeasurably depths I saw took my breath away, but he didn't answer my question. Instead, he laid an arm around my shoulder and told me I was very sweet and that beauty was in the eyes of the beholder.

We continued walking until we reached a bench where he asked me if I wanted to sit, and I replied that I did.

We must have sat there for a good five minutes before either one of us said a word. Finally, I broke the silence. "Is Satan real?"

I expected him to be surprised by my question, for I was surprised that I asked. "I'm sorry," I quickly said. "I don't know where that came from."

He reached back and took the band off his hair and let it fall gently to his shoulders, and stuck the band in his pants pocket. I thought he wasn't going to respond, but he leaned back against the bench and stretched his long legs out in front of him and said, "Yes! Satan is very real."

"Oh! Well, I guess the reason I asked is because a Satanist came in the library not long ago. He wore a necklace with what he called a sigil. I went home and looked it up. That is how I knew he was a Satanist."

"Were you afraid of him?"

"A little?"

"Why?"

"I guess because he's a Satanist."

"Therefore you judged him as being evil?"

Where was this going? I wasn't sure. "I suppose I did."

He sniggered faintly. "Judge not," he said.

"But he's a Satanist?"

The Bible doesn't say judge not except for Satanists."

That hit me like a ton of bricks. "Oh! You're right." I felt stupid then.

He apparently sensed it. "It's okay. Just about anyone would make the same mistake."

"But why would someone want to be a Satanist? Why would they want to sell their soul like that?"

He sat up straight then, showing no signs of irritation but only amusement by my questions. "First of all, Brenda – One does *not* sell their soul to Satan – One dedicates to Satan! As for the other half of your question, we all have our paths to follow. Some take the right-hand path, and some take the left. It is for each individual to discern which path is the one they want to take."

I was hesitant to ask, but I had to know. "Are *you* a Satanist?"

He grinned most charmingly. "Why do you ask?"

"You just seem to know so much about it."

"I have a thorough knowledge of ancient history. I know that much of the Bible was taken from other mythologies of the world and given Jewish characters. It was their way of controlling their people. Over time, it spread over the world into Christianity and Islamic beliefs. Of course, they added their own characters and stories." He must have noticed the perplexed expression on my face for he added, "Don't take my word for it. The truth is for everyone to seek; that is, if they really want to know. Do you?"

"Yes!"

"You work at the perfect place, Brenda. When you're not busy, start learning."

"I have read some books along that line… when I had the chance. But okay. I'll do that."

We were still close enough to the church that we could hear people coming out and leaving now.

"I guess I'd better get back before Greg realizes I'm not at the house."

"I'll walk you back."

"Thank you."

He escorted me to the corner where the park ended, and I ran across the street and onto the church grounds towards Greg's house. I could see Greg and Dad standing on the front porch of the church talking to a few remaining members. No one noticed me. At the door, I turned and waved to Erick, who waved back and then I went on inside. I did hold the door open a crack, for I was curious. I had to know. Sure enough, he simply vanished.

"Oh my God!" It appeared that my suspicions had been founded – He wasn't human! But who was he? More correctly, what was he?

*

Several weeks went by and I didn't see Erick anymore. My curiosity about him though had not diminished in the slightest. I did take his advice, though, and began reading everything I could on the old religions and mythologies of the world.

I came across The Epic of Gilgamesh and read it, and I couldn't help but consider the fact that it was the original story of the flood.

In the footnote of a Bible I was reading, I learned that the concept of the Virgin Mary was incorporated into the church because of the ancient goddess religions.

I also learned that Jesus' birthday wasn't really December twenty-fifth, but he was believed to be born in September.

The more I read, the more I wondered how much I had been taught all my life wasn't true. Was any of it true?

I didn't know what to believe.

I didn't dare take any of the books I was reading to Greg's, for I knew he would take one look at them and say they were works of the devil, even though they had been written by scholars and people who had spent their lives researching their materials. But that was the narrow-minded way of the churches. More and more it was clear to me that they wanted the masses to follow them blindly and not know the truth, for the truth might set them free!

It wasn't that I thought Christianity, Judaism and the Muslims all bad. The people didn't know any better. They were just following what they had been brainwashed to believe all their lives.

Also one had to appreciate the fact that some of the churches, synagogues and such, did do some good. Still, how much more harm had been done in the name of religion?

The Crusades came to mind. I thought of the Islamic wars that seemed to continuously rage overseas.

There were the Salem witch trials. Countless women had been murdered out of sheer panic caused from beliefs that were basically nothing but lies.

The magnitude of it all was just beginning to hit home to me. I almost felt suffocated by it all. I finally closed one book I was reading and not only put it away, I put all of them away.

I simply couldn't handle anymore right then. I needed time to process all of it, and it was so damn much to process!

Was there even a real God?

Then my mind went to Erick. I definitely now suspected he wasn't human. Something I had not told anyone.

But what was he?

*

Five paydays later I had enough money to rent my own apartment – looked more like a motel room when one walked in – but there was a kitchen and bathroom besides the little living room and bedroom combination– and luckily for me it was only a block from the library, across from the park, on the far side of the church. All were walking distance.

I paid my deposit and first and last month's rent to the middle-aged elderly couple that owned the apartments, but I hadn't moved in yet. They were painting the interior and putting in a new carpet. It would be a couple of days before I could move in. I didn't have to worry about furniture either. It was fully furnished. I hadn't told Greg yet. I sensed there would be an argument, so I was putting off telling him until the last minute.

There was no denying that Greg had been treating me well. For that, I was grateful, but it was more than apparent that he hoped I would stay, even though I was not sleeping with him, nor trying in any way to encourage him. I did fix his meals in return for his letting me stay there. But I think he took it as more, even though I told him otherwise.

It was Wednesday night and I decided to slip into the back of the church, as I was bored – service was three-quarters over – when a young woman just a few years older than I, went forward. I recognized her as Elsie Brown. She used to be a regular. I hadn't seen her in a while, but her husband came all the time. Right away she began babbling about how she'd sinned by not coming to church regularly with her husband and now she was paying for her sins. Her husband had been laid off work and she had just learned she had breast cancer.

Dad, of course, jumped right on it, laying his hands on her head and praying loudly; begging Jesus to forgive this woman of her iniquities so that her cancer would be healed.

Elsie fell right into it – tears gushing forth and crying out for God to forgive her.

Greg happened to look up and see me in the back of the church. He smiled; apparently thinking my being there was a good sign.

It wasn't. The whole charade, the entire scene, made me absolutely sick to my stomach.

I wanted to puke!

I couldn't handle it anymore. I left, walking as fast as I could. I had wanted to get an ice cream after church. So, I headed straight for Baskin Robbins. Maybe I should have taken my car, but I felt like walking. So I did.

I was a little surprised to see Nancy there, but what really blew my mind was she was sitting at one of the tables with the Satanist that had come in the library.

Immediately, she looked up and recognized me. "Brenda! Come on over. I want you to meet my new boyfriend."

The words, "You're what?" kind of caught in my throat as I made my way over to their table by the far right wall.

"Ah! The librarian," he said, smiling kind of strangely and mysteriously at the same time.

Nancy turned to him. "You've met then?"

"At the library," I replied, now standing beside her, staring at him staring back at me.

"Paul," he said, offering over his hand. "Name's Paul."

I was sure I hadn't forgotten his name. "I thought your name was Able?"

"Good memory," he replied, looking pleased. "Paul's my middle name. Why my mother named me Able is beyond me. I always hated that name… Able Paul," he sniggered.

"Maybe she thought that naming you that way would somehow help you to achieve whatever you wanted in life?"

He grinned. "Maybe.

"However, I believe that simply Paul definitely fits you better."

Jennifer told me to take a seat.

Paul pulled out a chair for me.

"Thanks."

Looking at me, Nancy said, "I've wanted to tell you how awful I feel about what my aunt did to you."

"Don't you mean to us? Seems to me that you were a victim too."

Nancy smiled at that. "Told you she was cool, Paul."

He puckered his lips slightly as though pondering and then shook his head in the affirmative. "Personally, I think Nancy's been way too nice about it."

"She's my aunt, Paul."

"Still. She's a total bitch."

"I won't argue with that."

I wanted to ask, but I wasn't certain how to go about it. I couldn't help wondering why a Wiccan would be hanging out with a Satanist. I started to speak but didn't.

Nancy picked up on my confusion right away. "I'm not a Wiccan anymore, Brenda."

"Oh?"

Paul interjected, "Nancy's known me for a while. Used to be afraid of me, weren't you?" he said, reaching over and squeezing her hand. "She used to have Mike wait on me when I came in. But now she knows the truth – That I wouldn't hurt her for anything." He scanned around as though to see if anyone was listening to our conversation, and then said, "Contrary to popular belief… we Satanists – spiritual Satanists, anyway – don't go around hurting people. We mind our own business, study and meditate and try to get the truth out to folks."

"The truth?"

He bobbed his head yes. "That the world has been deluded for centuries. That the Garden of Eden got so fucked up. Turned around. You see, Father Satan is the good God."

"That's right," Nancy agreed. "Paul's been teaching me… Showing me books, research. I didn't believe him at first, but now my *eyes* have been opened," she said with a proud smile and he winked at her.

I didn't understand until later exactly what she meant by that phrase.

He squeezed her hand again and let it go, leaning back in his chair and studying me. "So…What do you think, Brenda?"

"Like you said. Things got fucked up." I think that's the first time I ever said that word. Felt kind of weird, but I also had a sense of freedom as it left my lips.

Nancy laughed. "Good for you."

"You still with that preacher husband?" Paul asked.

"Just temporarily. I have an apartment, but can't move into it for a couple of days. They're painting and putting in a new carpet. Right now, Greg's been nice enough to let me stay at his place. Actually, he'd like me to stay period. But I'm not. We're done."

Nancy spoke, "Give me your phone number, Brenda. I'll call you and then you can save it. We'll keep in touch."

"Okay. I gave her my number, and she called me and I saved it.

Paul said, "When you get settled in that apartment, give Nancy a call. We'll all get together."

"I'll do that," I replied, feeling a sense of excitement about the whole thing. I was anxious to learn. I wanted to learn all I could about this 'spiritual' Satanism.

I glanced at the clock on the wall. It was after ten. "Well, I'm sure the church is about cleared out by now. Don't want Greg to think I got lost or something."

Paul hiked an eyebrow.

"I just don't want him looking for me. I'll be out of there soon enough. But for now, don't want any problems."

"Cool." Paul winked. "We got ya."

I ordered my coffee ice cream cone from Mike and waved to my friends, one old and one new, and left. I actually skipped all the way home. I felt like a little girl again.

My good mood died quickly. Greg was waiting for me. Instantly, I knew he was angry when he jerked the door open for me. "You were with that witch!"

Instantly riled – he'd been spying on me – I hotly retorted, "I went to grab an ice cream, Greg! I had no idea she was there. She just wanted to introduce me to her new boyfriend. I was being polite. And since when is it against the law to be friendly?" I stuck my ice cream cone in a short glass and set it in the freezer. I was too mad to enjoy it now.

Greg came up to me. I could readily see he wanted to say more, but thought better of it, since I was staring daggers at him.

"Okay. I'm sorry. You're right."

"Honestly. I had no idea she was back here. I wasn't going to be rude."

"Okay." He nodded. "I saw you head for Baskin Robbins and I thought of getting a cone myself, but then I saw you talking to Nancy … and … I guess I just kind of freaked out. I thought maybe you'd been in contact with her all along… That you'd been lying to me."

I stood there staring at him. He was hopeless. "Think about it Greg. You know I am moving out soon. What has been done has been done. And that was the first time I've seen Nancy since the incident in church. As far as our marriage goes, we're done. You know that. You *do* know that?"

He wriggled his head up and down. "Don't want to believe it. But yes. I know it is. Just a hard pill for me to swallow."

"It has been a pretty big pill for me too. All of it. But I can't be … I am not the person you want me to be. I'm sorry."

"We can still be friends, though? Right?"

"I hope so, Greg. I really hope so."

With a sideways nod, he said, "I guess that will have to be enough for now." He half grimaced and half smiled, looking around and then back to me. "Well, I'm tired. Going to take my shower and head for bed. Night."

"Night, Greg."

Chapter Eight

Try hard as I did, I could not sleep. I was excited about moving for one thing, but that was not foremost on my mind – Satan was!

I kept telling myself that there was no way Nancy and Paul – Able – whatever his name was, could be right.

I really didn't believe a demon could possess a person's body. Still, the mere thought of a demon terrified me.

Yet, why could I not get Satan out of my mind. I found myself sitting up on the couch and tossing the sheet back. It was hot too, which wasn't helping, but soon I would be in my little apartment with an AC that I fully intended to use.

Greg was sound asleep, so I slipped quietly over and opened up his laptop and went directly to the first Satanic website that I had come across earlier. Sure enough, there were instructions on how one could 'dedicate' to Satan.

Wasn't that the term Erick used? He did say dedicate, didn't he? And why did he know so much about Satan? Surely he wasn't a Satanist. He was just too nice for that! But then, I wasn't totally sure he was human. Still, he was a really good person. Hadn't he been my very best friend through all of this? But where was he now? I hadn't seen or heard from him in a while.

I thought about what I was doing. "Crap! I am losing it!" Quickly, I closed out the website, cleared my cookies and history, went to pee and then returned to bed.

Only I had one dream after another, and all were strange and weird and unclear to me: symbols, colors, letters that I didn't understand, which I later came to recognize as runes.

I woke up the next morning in a cold sweat and realized that Greg was staring at me from the kitchen. "You okay?" he inquired, as he sipped on his coffee. "You've been mumbling in your sleep for a good half hour."

"Just really crazy dreams."

"Want to share?"

I sat up, placed my feet on the floor and stood. "I really can't remember what they were about. Just that they were so strange. Kept seeing bright colors floating around in cloud-like forms, and little lights flashing here and there, and then there were these strange letters that I didn't' understand."

"Hmmm," he said, rinsing out his cup in the sink. He faced me. "I need to get over to the church right now. Have a couple coming in for marriage counseling."

It was all I could do to stifle a laugh, but I managed. I didn't want to piss him off at that particular moment. "Oh! Okay," was all I said.

"Maybe later, if you remember enough, you can tell me more about your dreams."

"Yeah. Sure. Maybe," I said, smiling vaguely, but figuring no way in hell.

He grabbed up his Bible from the coffee table and bid me a good morning and quickly left.

I let out a sigh of relief. He would be at the church most of the day. And I was anxious to see if I could start moving into my apartment.

Soon as I was dressed and had my makeup on, I gave the Sharps a call. Adam answered in his somewhat gruff but friendly voice. He said there was a delay and it would be one more day before I could move in. I was a little disappointed, but he was very apologetic. Said there was a leak at the toilet base and it needed a new flange. He was apologetic for the delay, but they couldn't get the plumber there until after five. He hoped that I wouldn't mind waiting one more day.

I politely thanked him, knowing he was just being a good landlord, but I was definitely disappointed. I glanced around, doing a mental inventory. I had everything ready to go. My clothes were ready and packed. And I had a few dishes that I had picked up here and there, not wanting to take any from Greg, packed in a medium sized box and waiting in the trunk of my car. I let out a deep sigh and decided to take a walk. It was still early morning, and not too hot yet.

Naturally, I ended up at the park.

It had been so long since I had seen Erick; I was beginning to wonder if he was still around. Every time I realized a jogger was coming I'd look up immediately hoping it was him. And it wasn't long and I got a surprise, instead of Erick coming down the runners' path, Paul was. He had on black jogging shorts with white stripes on the sides, and a white tee-shirt. There was a black sweatband around his forehead. That necklace still hung around his neck though. It was hard for me to not stare at it.

Seeing me, he smiled right away and stopped running and approached. "Hey!" he said, as he came up to my bench. "Didn't occur to me that I might see you here. How's it going?"

"Okay, I guess. Disappointed though. Can't move into my apartment until tomorrow. Toilet sprang a leak and the landlord's having it fixed. But he can't get the plumber out until later."

"That sucks," he said, wiping his cheeks with the bottom of his shirt. I couldn't help but notice his well-defined, six-pack abs.

"I guess I'll just deal with it," I replied, glad he'd let his shirt down. His well-formed body was a bit distracting. It was no wonder Nancy was nuts about him.

"Look at it this way. Better now than after you move in."

"You're right." I realized he wasn't bad looking at all, with those dark, hooded eyes that sparkled mysteriously and that broad forehead. He had a really cute, quirky kind of grin that I'm sure that many a girl could find unnerving. I was certain that Nancy did. Probably melted her heart. "Where's Nancy?"

"Oh! She got her job back. In fact, that was one of the reasons we were at Baskin Robbins when you came in. She was hoping that they had a spot for her… Turns out that the Hispanic woman that took her place had just quit. They were glad Nancy was back, rehired her on the spot."

"That's awesome!"

"We thought so."

"Mind if I ask what you do for a living?"

"I work from my apartment," he nodded towards the same apartment building where mine was.

"You live there?" I asked in surprise.

"Sure do." His smile grew. "Don't tell me that's where you're moving to?"

"Yes! The last one on this end. I think I lucked out. I can actually park my car beside it and not under the long canopy like the others. I have my own private overhang, shaded by shrubs on the street side. So no one can see my car from the road clearly."

"Absolutely awesome!" He high-fived me.

"Does Nancy live close?"

"I'd say. She's with me. We live together now."

"Cool!"

"And to finish answering your original question, I work on my computer. I build websites for folks with less technological expertise," he said with that quirky little grin.

"Is there good money in it?"

"I try not to be too expensive. Depending on what a client wants, I charge anywhere from a hundred and fifty to five hundred dollars. And I am a fast worker." He nodded and wiped his face again, as the sweat was rolling in beads down his cheeks. "I make enough to pay rent, keep my Mazda in gas and eat all the pizza we want."

"Sounds wonderful."

He stood then. "Well, I should finish off my run for the morning. I have a website in the works that I need to get back to."

"Thanks for the chat, Paul."

"You're mighty welcome. I'm sure we'll see you soon." He took off running then.

"Well, that was interesting," I said to myself. Deciding that it was getting too hot to stay out in the sun, and the park was filling with mothers and their preschoolers in the shaded areas were the swings and slides were. I headed on back to Greg's.

*

I had hoped to have most of my things moved in my apartment before I told Greg, but since things had been delayed another day, I figured that I might as well tell him. After all, the apartment was mine. I just couldn't start taking my things over until the next morning.

I figured Greg would come in for lunch, so I made tuna sandwiches and iced tea; something we both liked a lot. It was one of the few things we had in common. But liking tuna sandwiches and iced tea isn't exactly sufficient reason for staying in an otherwise dysfunctional marriage.

He was all smiles and happy with himself when he breezed in and saw his lunch waiting. "Thanks, Brenda!" He went straight to the sink and washed his hands.

I had already eaten, so picked up my plate and glass, meeting him at the sink, and set them on the counter to wait until he finished.

He turned, still smiling, as he wiped his hands on a paper towel. I walked away to sit on the sofa, but he said, "If you have a minute, why don't you sit with me while I eat?"

Wanting to keep him in a good mood, I replied okay and pulled out a chair to his right.

"You know," he said, "I feel really good about the couple this morning. I think we managed to get somewhere. The wife seems eager to do whatever she must to make their marriage work, and I believe her husband is willing too. Definitely they are God-fearing people"

I was a bit apprehensive as to where this was going, but I kept my mouth shut. And I could not help but linger on 'God-fearing'. Why should one have to fear a truly loving god?

He took a few bites of his sandwich and drank some tea. I could almost see the wheels of thought turning in his head. He took a few more bites, swallowed and looked at me squarely. "Brenda, I think we could still make this work."

Shit! "Greg—."

"I know," he said. "I know you don't believe we can. But what God hath joined together, let no man put asunder."

Now he was quoting from the traditional marriage ceremony.

"I am a man, Brenda! I still love you! And I think you still have feelings for me." He tilted his brow forward inquisitively. "You do, don't you?"

I pondered as to whether I should tell him now that I was ready to move out. He knew I'd been packing, but he didn't know that I had an apartment yet.

"Brenda?"

"Greg, I'll always care for you. That's not it. To put it simply – We are mismatched."

His faced twisted in confusion. "What? Mismatched? What an absurd thing to say."

"Not from my viewpoint. You… You are into the church. The church is your life! And that's okay – for you! I know I married you knowing you were a minister. In spite of the fact that Mom warned me not to make the same mistakes she did. But I was so crazy about you I couldn't see the bigger picture.

He was only hearing what he wanted to hear. "You do love me! I knew you did!"

"I do love you, Greg, but not the way you want me to. Not the way you need me to." My frustration was blossoming into anger. "I can't be a subservient slave to a life where I am miserable all the time. *There is no time for me! I need… I want time for me!*" I realized I was yelling and hoped Dad hadn't heard.

"That's the devil talking through you! You're not yourself!"

"No! I am the one talking here, Greg! No devil involved!" I turned away from him in frustration. "Crap! Why on Earth did I not listen to Mom?"

We both stood there for several minutes just staring one another down but not saying a word.

Then there was a loud knock on the door and Dad's voice came through. "Everything okay in there?"

"You promised me he'd stay away, Greg!"

"I did. But this has gotten out of hand." He rushed over to the door and opened it and let Dad in.

"Don't do this!" I said, shaking so hard I could barely stand.

"I've figured it out," Greg said to Dad. "She's possessed!"

Dad's eyes immediately fell on me, as he pondered over Greg's words. "You're right! Why did I not see it?"

"What the hell!" I yelled. This was not good. Not good at all. Their faces were like crazed animals. They had let themselves be convinced that I was possessed. I scanned my surroundings looking for an opening where I could run through them, but they were closing in on me. I made a dash for it anyway, but Dad caught me. And though he was older, he was taller than Greg by about three inches (Greg was only five-foot-eleven) and more muscular. Kept himself in shape. He held me so tight I could hardly breathe.

"Get something to tie her hands behind her back," Dad ordered.

"Right!"

"You're freakin' kidding me!" I screamed in horror.

Greg came right back with one of his leather belts and tied my hands while Dad held me.

I screamed. I yelled. I cursed profanities that I hadn't even been aware that I knew until that moment. Of course, now that I think about it, it didn't help my case at all. It wouldn't have mattered though. They were already convinced.

While Dad held me, Greg got on the phone and began calling all the parishioners and telling them I needed an exorcism, for everyone to get to the church as soon as possible.

"Seriously? You're doing this?" I screamed at Greg.

He looked at me with perplexed but sad eyes and said, "I'm sorry, Brenda. But this has to be done. I realize that now. It's because you hung out with those witches. You went and got yourself possessed. We should have known."

"I don't have a freakin' demon! I just want to be treated decently! That does not make me evil!"

Soon church members were knocking at the door. They were mostly the elderly members who were retired and didn't have jobs to go to, but there were a few younger members that were off for one reason or the other.

I realized that my screaming wasn't getting me anywhere, so I shut up and just glared at all their 'concerned' faces. I could have spit nails at all of them, had I been able to.

I was never so humiliated in my entire life when Dad and Greg dragged me across the yard and into the church with the others following behind. I didn't dare look to the right or left. I didn't want to look at all. I just wanted to die right then and there. Still, I knew that if I came out of this alive, that things were going to be different – A lot different!

You've seen in movies where a person, supposedly, is having a demon exorcised, and they spit at the priest. Well, I totally get it now. I spit in Dad's face, and I spit in Greg's. At that moment, I hated them both with every sinew in my body and, when I did chance to look at a couple of the assisting church members, I hated them too. The anger seared through me like a hot, all-consuming flame.

The ridiculous nightmare seemed to me to go on for hours.

Dad kept yelling at me as though he were talking to a demon, demanding the demon to come out of me.

Of course there was no demon. They were just freakin' nuts on a crazed high.

I fought them for as long as I could, but after a while, I was too exhausted. I felt as though I was going to pass out. In fact, I think I did a time or two, but then someone would slap my face and futilely order the demon to come out again.

I couldn't take it anymore. I knew the only way to get out of this now was to pretend to let the demon go. So, with what energy I could muster, I yelled more profanities at my Dad and Greg, and then feigned passing out momentarily, before waking up and suddenly went all sweet and innocent, acting like I had no clue what had been going on.

I must have played the part good, for Dad and Greg suddenly started thanking Jesus for saving me, and I just closed my eyes. Then I actually did pass out.

I woke up around midnight on Greg's bed! Next to Greg!

The freakin' imbecile actually believed that things were going to be okay now. I mouthed, "Oh my God!" I lay there for several minutes considering what to do. I know that I didn't want to be there a second longer than necessary.

I waited a few minutes listening to Greg's deep breathing. He was definitely asleep. I figured he was probably exhausted too, from the long ordeal at the church. I ever so slowly and carefully shoved back my covers and slipped my legs around to the side of the bed and sat up. I waited a few seconds. Greg was still sleeping. I stood, waited another few moments, and then satisfied that I could continue undetected, I grabbed my keys and cell phone off the dresser drawers and tiptoed to the living room. My box of things was still there. I didn't even bother to change clothes. I figured the sooner I got out of there, the better. It was past midnight. So I figured that I could go on to my apartment now.

I quietly let myself out the door and glanced at my car. It too was still there. I had held the fear that they had hid it from me somewhere, but they hadn't. I can't say how thankful for that I was. I let out another sigh of relief and hurried over to it. I unlocked the door on the passenger side and tossed my box in, ran around and let myself in, and wasted not a second in starting up my car.

A light came on in Greg's bedroom. He knew! I peeled out of the driveway backwards, knocking over the garbage can. I didn't care. I drove away as quickly as I could. And boy was I glad that Greg didn't know I had an apartment, and had no clue that it was only a few blocks away.

I took a chance and kept my headlights off, so he couldn't follow me easily with his eyes. I even drove several blocks out of the way at first, hoping to make sure he had lost sight of me. I couldn't believe that I had actually made it so far without any cops noticing me driving around without my headlights.

After about twenty minutes, I decided that I had circled the park a sufficient number of times and headed straight for my place.

Soon as I arrived, I eased my car under my apartment's private canopy where it was shielded by the shrubs, grabbed my box and let myself into my new home. Ran back out and got my things out of the trunk, locked my door and then I went to my bedroom.

My bedroom! Yes! My bed!

It wasn't made. No sheets or anything. I didn't care. Free at last, I turned the light out and threw myself across the bare mattress and fell into a blissful slumber

Chapter Nine

Morning brought glorious sunshine streaming through my window – Albeit a little too brightly. I had forgotten one important thing: Curtains! I picked up my iPhone and checked the time. Only a quarter of five. I didn't really want to get up yet, but it was much, much too bright to go back to sleep, so I gave in to my circumstances and pulled myself out of bed.

After I dressed, peed, brushed my teeth and washed my face, I made my way to my little kitchen. The box was still perched on top of the counter by the sink. I dug out my coffeemaker, happy that I had brought along some coffee in a plastic sandwich bag, and two more bags with some coffee creamer and sugar. At least I could have my coffee. I would go to the store after I got my brain revived and in gear and buy whatever groceries I figured I could get by with until I got paid the following Thursday.

I sat down to my tiny kitchen table with the old fashioned, red and white checkered tablecloth, that was furnished with only two chairs, but I didn't care. Figured I wouldn't have a lot of company. Don't know why I thought that. I just did. I suppose I can attribute it to the fact that being raised in such a heavy 'Christian' environment; I had had a very sheltered life growing up. Therefore, with the exception of church members, I never really had many friends.

Done with my coffee, I grabbed my phone and made my grocery list. I planned on eating TV dinners, salads and sandwiches mostly, and was happy that the apartment had a small microwave furnished. It was brand new, according to my landlord.

I had one small iron skillet and a medium pan for boiling eggs, water, or whatever else I might need it for. I had a couple of tablespoons, two teaspoons, two butter knives, one steak knife, one paring knife, and two forks. I also had a disposable set of salt and pepper that I had purchased a few months back, thinking we might use them on a picnic. That never happened, but I was grateful for them now. They were unopened and new as the day I bought them.

I would need milk, eggs and butter. Those were first on my list; bread of course, and lunch meat for those sandwiches. Then I jotted down peanut butter at the bottom. Didn't want to forget that. I love peanut butter. That meant I needed crackers too. Then I thought I might want soup, and toilet paper, and soap. The longer I sat there, the longer my list got. I finally just closed my phone and stuck it in my jeans pocket. I had allowed only so much for groceries and I didn't want to overspend.

So, with list in hand, I headed for Safeway, but not the one closest to us. I was afraid I might run into Dad or Greg there. There was another one about a mile away. I headed for it instead.

As I meandered around the store – didn't know where anything was, and I had taken the day off and was in no hurry– the horrors of the evening before kept popping in my head. I got chills just remembering how Dad and Greg had taken me by my wrists and literally dragged me across the yard while all the parishioners gaped in warped interest. It sure as hell seemed warped to me, anyway. I even had bands of bruises around both wrists that were quite noticeable.

How could people who were supposed to be good, upright, caring folk stand by as though they were simply watching an act in the circus and do nothing to help the person being submitted to such humiliation and embarrassment?

No one that fit my definitions of good could.

Just then, I realized that I was staring at a display of scented candles. "Hmmm," I pondered, suddenly getting an idea that I would have never believed possible – To dedicate my soul to Satan!

"Oh my God!" I said to myself, and suddenly pushed my basket on and around to the next aisle. How could I have possible thought that?

I realized my hands were trembling, and my thoughts returned to the evening before. Then I thought of Paul. He was a Satanist, but he sure seemed like an awfully nice guy from what I knew of him.

I'm not sure how long I stood there, but a young black woman came up behind me and politely asked me if I was okay. Surprised, I looked at her and asked why.

"Because you've been standing there just staring at the shelf for a good ten minutes. It was like you were in a trance or something. I just wanted to make sure you were okay."

I bobbed my head apologetically. "Sorry. I just moved, and I'm not sure exactly what all I need." I held up my list. "I'm still not certain I have everything on here."

"I've been there and done that," she replied. "Frankly, I hate moving." She smiled broadly then, and I realized she was very pretty with her big brown eyes, black hair cut in a pixyish style, and large hoop earrings. And she had an hourglass figure that many a female would die for. What's more, the red, short-sleeved top and new jeans she wore fit her perfectly.

"Yes. It is kind of the pits… And thank you for caring enough to see if I was okay."

"Don't thank me, sugar. Just doing what anyone should do." She went to pushing her basket forward. "You have a good day now."

"You too!" I replied. I felt a little better. I guess my faith in humanity had been restored somewhat. I continued with my shopping.

Once home, I put my groceries away and made myself a glass of instant iced tea. Wasn't the greatest, but it was hot out and I direly wanted a cold drink that wasn't soda. For me, when I am really hot and thirsty, tea trumps soda any day of the week. Don't get me wrong, though, I am a big cola-holic. I did put some tea bags in some boiling water to steep, though, for later.

Again, Satanism popped into my mind. I remembered several Satanic websites that I wanted to look into more. I didn't have a computer or an iPad, but I had an iPhone. I went online and tried to look the websites up, but it was too tedious to read so much information on the phone. I needed a computer.

I had taken the day off for moving, but there was a whole line of public computers at the library. I finished up my iced tea and headed straight there.

Of course, right away, Mrs. Peters wondered what I was doing there when I had taken the day off to move. I didn't want to tell her that I was interested in researching Satanism – old habits die hard as well as old fear – so I told her I needed to email a friend. Something I could have done on my phone, but she didn't know that. The library was pretty busy, but there was one computer available.

I took a seat and brought up the website. Wouldn't you know? I must have had a die-hard church-goer next to me to the right. The second she noticed the black pages with blood-red texts and the inverted star, she gave me a really wary look, snatched up some papers she'd been taking notes on and left her computer, not even bothering to log off. Of course, I did it for her. The computers were supposed to be cleared once one was through with what they were doing. Then there was a young Hispanic man about my age to my left. He raised an eyebrow and I could almost feel the cold come over him. He didn't stay at his computer long either. But he did have the decency to log off and clear out.

I sat there for a moment, feeling my cheeks grow warm. This was too uncomfortable. There were far too many people with really narrow-minded and negative attitudes about Satanism. I know. Just a short time ago I had been one of them!

I got off the computer right away. Bid Mrs. Peters goodbye and left. Now I was upset. I wanted – needed – to know more.

What was I to do?

Then it hit me. I slapped myself up beside my head. Paul! That was it. He said he worked from home. And he was just a few doors down from me. Soon as I reached my apartment, I put my purse away, and then walked on down to his and Nancy's apartment.

He answered the door immediately. His normally neat hair was in disarray, and he looked tired, but he welcomed me inside with a big smile and offered me a cold Coke, which I graciously accepted.

Nancy was at work and would be for several more hours. He seemed glad for company, said he was tired of sitting at the computer and had been considering taking a walk in the park anyway, until I knocked.

"So … What's up, girl? I'm getting some anxious vibes from you. Did you get moved in?"

"Well, not everything is put away, but I have everything inside."

"That's the main thing."

"I'll get to the point. You told me you're a Satanist."

He had been leaning forward, elbows on his knees, but he suddenly sat up straight and laid an arm on the back of the sofa.

I sat opposite him on a recliner that had seen better days, but he had confessed it was far too comfortable to get rid of. And he was right.

"Yes! I am." He eyed me curiously, introspectively. "Why?"

"I… I'm considering dedicating to Satan."

"Wow! That one I didn't expect coming. Not from you."

Confused, I asked, "What do you mean?"

"I know you've had some really hard times with your Dad and hubby and all that, but you've been a Christian all your life." He held up an outward Palm. "Don't get me wrong. I think it's awesome, if that is what you really want. I am sure Father Satan… Enki … will welcome you into the family with open arms. But…and that is a big but … you need to be one-hundred percent sure that this is what you want."

"I think it is."

He shook his head slightly. "Not think, Brenda. You have to know! Once you dedicate to Father Satan it is permanent. No wishy-washy changing your mind. It is forever! Not just this lifetime, but any lifetimes you have to come!"

"Huh?" This I had not expected. "You mean like in reincarnation?"

"Exactly!"

"Oh! I hadn't thought about that, I guess."

"I'm pretty sure you don't believe in reincarnation, having been brought up in the church. Am I right?"

"I've always wondered about it. I know that there are other religions that do. I just didn't realize that Satanists did."

"Not all Satanists, Brenda. Just spiritual Satanists. There are some who call themselves Satanists … like the LeVayans. But they don't even really believe that Father Satan is a real being."

"Oh? Seems like I heard that before."

"Maybe Nancy ran it by you?"

"Maybe. Or I read it on the internet." What he was saying was pretty heavy. Once a Satanist, it wasn't only for this lifetime but forever! "Wow!" I shrugged my shoulders. "But you believe Satan is real?"

"I don't believe it – I know it! He has spoken to me more than once. He is a real being. And he truly loves His children. What's more, He actually answers us when we need him. He's not like the other one – the one you've followed all your life – the one that lets you beg and pray and cry and carry on and maybe, just maybe, you will get an answer, but most often you won't. And even if you do, it might be twenty years later. No! Father Satan has our backs. He is with us one hundred percent."

"Again – wow! Doesn't sound anything like what I have been raised to believe."

"Unfortunately, that is the big lie to the world. Satan means adversary. But he's not *our* adversary. He is the other one's enemy. The whole thing got turned around backwards a long time ago. In the Garden of Eden, Father wanted to help us… Wanted to teach us… Wanted mankind to grow and become great. The other one wanted to keep us ignorant slaves."

"Yes. I believe Nancy said something like that."

"To break it down in a few words – The Christians teach that Satan is the father of lies."

"Yes! That's what I've always been told."

"Get this, Brenda. Swallow it good – the God you've been taught to worship is the true adversary, the liar. And my God is of the truth. Hence: God is Satan and Satan is God!"

I think my mouth dropped about a mile. It felt like it anyway. "Oh shit!" Nothing ever hit me so profoundly. I was suddenly sick and had to throw up.

Paul understood perfectly and ran ahead of me to open the bathroom door for me. I threw up my iced tea, Coke, what little else I had had that day. Afterwards, I just sat there in the floor.

Paul was kind enough to rinse out a washcloth, wring it out and place it on the back of my neck. He sat there with me in the bathroom floor while I shook like a leaf.

I'm not sure how long I sat there, but I finally managed to get a grip on myself. I turned my face towards his. "I think I'm okay now."

"You're sure?"

I bobbed my head yes.

"Okay. Tell you what. You go ahead in the living room and sit down. Put your feet up on the coffee table. Better yet, take the chair and lean it back. It has a rest for your feet. I'll clean up the mess here."

"Oh! I should clean it. Gee!"

"Not a problem. I used to take care of my little brother and sister when Mom worked nights. Seems like they were always getting sick. Dad left us when I was ten. Sam and Taylor were two and three. My brother and sister."

"I didn't know that."

"Of course you didn't. Now go ahead. I'll be out in a minute. And don't feel badly. It's okay. It really is."

"You're the greatest! But I'm so embarrassed. No wonder Nancy is with you."

"Oh! I have my faults. But she loves me."

"I know she does." I turned and went on to the living room then and did as he said.

A few minutes later Paul returned. I did notice that he had stopped long enough to comb his hair. He leaned against the back of the sofa. "So, if you think you want to dedicate to Father Satan, I think that is great. More than great. Awesome! But it is a very serious undertaking."

"I realize that. And why do you refer to him as Father Satan part of the time and Father Enki part of the time?"

"Ummm… First, to answer your question: Satan is really more of a title, adversary, as we've mentioned before. His name is Ea. Enki means Lord of the Earth. However, Enki has kind of become a name for Him over time."

"Oh?"

"As far as you understanding or realizing what this is all about, I'm sure you do to an extent, but only to an extent. There are things that are going to happen that I am sure you are not prepared for."

"Like what?"

He kind of laughed and then apologized. "Not laughing at you or your question. It's just that no one is ever really prepared. Because there is no way one can prepare you."

"I don't follow."

"I don't expect you to. All I can say is… if you do go through with it, expect the unexpected."

"Okay," I replied, vaguely nodding.

"It is never the same with two people. Each one goes through it a little differently. Primarily, because everyone is unique in his or her own way. Therefore we experience things in a truly personal way that is all ours."

I still wasn't totally getting what he was trying to convey, but I kind of got the drift. At least, I thought I did. "Then what should I do? Any suggestions?"

"Ever meditate?"

"Tried a time or two, but I didn't seem to get anywhere with it."

"It takes time. Relaxation is the key." He stood and asked me to wait a minute. He ran over to his desk and took some papers out of a drawer and brought them back to me. "Here. I printed these up for Nancy when she first turned. She has it down pat now, so I am sure she is okay with you using them."

"What are they? Instructions?"

"Yes. Basic meditations: How to build your aura, your energy... things like that. You try meditating for a few days and study the website thoroughly, and then think over all that I said, and then if you still want to dedicate to Father Satan, I will be happy to lone you what you need."

"What's that?"

"Candles, incense, oils, silver bowl, chalice. And you can get those things on your own, if you want? You can order your supplies online. I normally don't lone them out, but you are a friend of Nancy's and one of mine now. So, if you decide to go ahead and dedicate, I don't want you to have to wait for them to come in the snail-mail."

"That's really kind of you."

He raised his hand slightly in gesture. "Hey! I'll be tickled to the bone if you do decide to dedicate. I know Father Satan will be overjoyed to have a new member to his family."

I pushed the seat forward and set my feet on the floor. "I feel a lot better already. I know you have work to do, and I've taken up enough of your time. And," I rolled my eyes, "I still have more than a few things to unpack and put away."

"Yeah. I hate moving."

"Doesn't everyone?" I smiled. "Thank you so much, Paul."

"You're sure you're okay now?" he asked, now standing too and shadowing me to the door.

"Again, I am so sorry about the tossing my cookies thing."

"Not a problem." He laid a gentle hand on my shoulder.

I opened the door. "Thanks again!"

"Honestly, I was glad for the break. And don't hesitate to come around...whether it is to visit or if you need something."

"And same to you and Nancy," I replied. I left then, feeling a little confused, still, but a whole lot better about things.

Once home, I looked over the papers he gave me and set them aside. I would study them later. I was antsy and not sure what I wanted to do at that exact moment. There were more websites on Satanism, but, from what I could tell, Joy of Satan was the most comprehensive.

I needed time to think. Still, some things I believe are concrete. For instance, Enki being the true Father of mankind: That, after much speculation, I truly came to realize and believe.

It was like a breath of fresh air to my spirit!

It took me a couple of days, for I wanted to be certain beyond all doubt, but I finally made my decision. I was going to dedicate to Ea-Enki aka Satan.

Chapter Ten

Several weeks passed in which I did considerable, extensive research. I read *The Lost Book of Enki* and *The 12ᵗʰ Planet* by Zecharia Sitchin, but I wasn't sticking to one resource. I also read a Babylonian version of *The Epic of Gilgamesh.* I read *Chariots of the Gods* by Erich Van Däniken. Then I even read some of the works of D. M. Murdock aka Archaya S. I had to stop. Eyestrain was getting the better of me.

Paul and Nancy had been absolutely awesome in their support of me while I was exploring and learning as much as I could. They had me over for dinner a couple of times. In return, I had them over for pizza on several occasions, as I didn't have many dishes or cookware. Paper plates were just great for Pizza though.

If I had questions that I couldn't find in the books, they did their best to answer them for me. I was more than appreciative of their help and was truly grateful to have them for my friends.

I wondered about Erick, though. I had not seen him in a long time; not jogging, not feeding the squirrels in the park, nothing. Had he moved? Honestly, I kind of missed him. I truly believed that there was something very special about him.

Had I imagined seeing him disappear that night? The more I thought about it, I was certain that he had just stepped into the shadows or something. He was human. Had to be. Why I had thought him otherwise kind of baffled me now. I figured it must have been all the stress I was under. Regardless, I hoped that I would see him again. I really did miss him.

For personal reasons, I ordered the paperback version of *The Lost Book of Enki*, of which I now considered my Bible. For I now considered it more accurate and more truthful than anything the Bible had to offer. After all, it was taken directly from Sumerian texts, the oldest known civilization of man. Though there are some who question its authenticity, there are other civilizations that point to this Aryan race of beings; one of the main ones being Egypt.

To top it all off, I had watched a few episodes of *Ancient Aliens* in the past when Greg or my dad wasn't around. I knew they would have put me through the mill had they known I even considered watching it. However, I found some *Ancient Alien* DVDs at the library. One of which was about Satan. I borrowed a DVD player from Mrs. Peters and took it home. When I finished watching that, I needed no more convincing. The whole theme of the show was that Satan or whatever one might want to call him seemed to have been maligned all through the years, that maybe he wasn't such a bad guy after all. The obloquy that Satan had suffered all these eons was simply mindboggling.

There was so much more too. I hadn't even touched on many lengthy works by Robert Graves and James Frazer.

That did it!

How could one not pay attention to all these learned men and women? How could one avoid the works of these scholars? The proof was there. All one had to do was open their eyes!

I needed no more convincing.

I know that others might draw different conclusions to all that I had read. However, from my perspective, I could not draw any other conclusion; Enki was the true creator of man!

I didn't want to waste any more time. I was determined to dedicate and start my new life as a Satanist. Or, more accurately, an Enkiite!

I had found all the supplies I needed online and they had been delivered to me several days before. It had been nice of Paul to offer letting me use theirs, but I wanted my own. I felt it was more personal that way. I was ready.

I had assumed that Paul and Nancy would want to be with me when I dedicated, and ran down to their apartment that Friday evening to tell them I was ready, but I was surprised when Paul told me that it was a really personal thing, that I would be better off doing in it alone, in private.

Nancy agreed. But Paul did say they would come if I really wanted them too. Nancy agreed with a nod.

"If you say it's better to do it alone, then I will do it alone." I replied, more nervous now.

"It's nothing to be afraid of," Paul said with assurance. "You're not going to disappear into some black hole somewhere."

"And you're not going to burst into flames," Nancy promised.

"You will definitely notice things," Paul added. "Like I told you before, it's not the same with everyone. Everyone is different. And it might not be immediately, but then again, it might be. Just expect the unexpected."

"Okay," I replied with a hesitant shrug.

Seeing my uneasiness, Nancy assured me that it was going to be okay.

Then Paul added, "What I told you before – the only thing to fear is fear itself! Don't be afraid. There is nothing to fear!"

I breathed out heavily. "Okay. Thanks, both of you!"

They hugged me and wished me luck, and I turned and ran back to my apartment where I had everything already set up.

I closed and locked my door and went over to a little end table that I had purchased at the nearest thrift store and set it in the far corner of my little living room. I had painted it black, and had a dark blue, felt cloth laid over it, as Paul had told me that blue was one of Satan's colors. I had a red candle and a black candle. And, of course, my bowl to burn my dedication paper was silver and my chalice was silver. I also had grape juice in my chalice to drink during my dedication.

I had a needle sterilized and ready to prick my left forefinger, and an alcohol wipe ready to wipe my finger once I was done letting blood for the dedication.

I had taken a clean piece of copy paper and cut it into quarters. On one of the quarters I wrote my dedication to Satan, forsaking all and any previous allegiances. I performed a little invocation that Paul instructed to me, and I drank from my chalice and set it aside, and then I pricked my finger. Nothing. I pricked it several more times, because blood did not flow that easily.

I was beginning to think I wasn't going to get any blood out when I finally took a deep breath and stuck my finger really hard with the needle. It worked! Blood oozed out. I stuck the end of my pen in the blood and then wrote my name the best I could. It wasn't all in blood, but it was covered with blood. Jennifer and Paul had both assured me that it would be okay, as it was very hard to get enough blood to sign ones entire signature, that as long as there was some, it was all that mattered.

I then took my lighter and lit it, sticking the flame under one of the bottom corners of the paper and held it over the silver bowl with tongs to keep from burning myself. And I was immediately grateful that Jennifer had told me to do this when I saw the paper engulfed in flames so quickly. I dropped it into the silver bowl. In mere seconds it was smoldering ashes.

Done!

I dropped down to my knees, as Jennifer and Paul had instructed me to do, and observed a quiet moment in respect for Father Satan. I was shaking from head to foot though. I couldn't help it. I had done what I wanted to do, what I felt was the right thing to do, but I couldn't help all the years of brainwashing.

I was terrified!

I kept telling myself that I would be okay. Nothing was going to happen to me. Paul and Nancy had done it and they were fine. "The only thing you have to fear, Brenda," I said to myself, rising to my feet, "is fear itself!"

I poured water in the bowl. It was night now. So no one would see. I went straight outside to the other side of the canopy where my car was parked and poured the water, along with the ashes, onto the ground under the first shrub. Paul had told me not to pour it down the sink, out of respect. I then promptly went back inside and rinsed out the bowl in the kitchen sink and placed it under the sink, as well as my chalice, after cleaning it, and the rest of my supplies.

I scanned my surroundings. Everything looked the same. I felt the same. Sort of. I was still shaking and still kind of scared. But I kept repeating what I had been told. "Nothing to fear but fear itself." And I went to bed.

To my surprise, I fell instantly to sleep and slept really sound. I didn't even have any dreams that I could recall when I woke up the next morning.

Certainly no demons had come in the night to steal me away. Something that I had kind of feared in the back of my mind in spite of all that I had read and been told by my new friends – that demons were really very warm and loving beings, that they were very helpful and kind. However, it would be better if I referred to them as gods, as that was what they truly were. I had to keep reminding myself of all that I had recently learned. It wasn't easy, not after all the years and years of constant brainwashing.

I knew it was going to take some time.

I dressed, ate a quick breakfast of Cheerio's, had a cup of coffee and went to work. It was just like any other day. So what had I been so afraid of?

Still, throughout the day, I kind of halfway expected something to happen. But nothing did.

*

A week went by with nothing out of the ordinary taking place. In one respect I was truly beginning to relax, but on the other, I was feeling kind of let down. I had been told that my life would change, not only completely, but possibly drastically. But nothing out of the ordinary had happened.

It was Saturday and I was scheduled to work only until noon. I thought I might go down and visit with Nancy and Paul, but when I knocked on their door there was no answer. That was when I realized Paul's black Dodge Ram wasn't parked in its designated spot. Neither was Nancy's red Toyota.

"Dammit!" I hissed and went back to my apartment. I tried to watch television, but there wasn't anything on that caught my attention. Bummed out, I decided to take a nap and laid down on my bed, pulling the blue, lightweight blanket I had across the bottom of my bed over me, and over my face to block out the daylight.

I'm not sure exactly how long I slept, but when I opened my eyes, it was beginning to get dark outside. It was late summer, so it had to be around eight. I rolled over to check the clock on my nightstand and found myself staring into the face of this dwarf. I screamed. He simply grinned kind of mysteriously, as though he had some wonderful secret, and disappeared.

"What the hell?" I sprang out of bed and frantically scanned my surroundings. *I had not imagined him! I hadn't!*

But where had he gone? And who was he? One of the things I did notice about him was that he had a hood over his head, like he was wearing a hoodie. But it was warm – outside and in. It only took me a minute to search my little apartment, being as there was only the one bedroom, bathroom, living room and kitchen.

I wondered if he had run outside. But my door was still locked. There was no way he could have gone outside and locked the door from the other side without a key. I reached in my pocket. My apartment key was still on my chain.

"What in blazes is going on?"

Then it hit me that maybe, just maybe, I had still been kind of in a dream when I awoke, and I just thought I saw him. The more I thought about it, I realized that the little man wasn't totally solid. He was kind of see-through, although I could see his twinkling eyes and his body and the hoodie he wore. Yes. I decided that was the explanation. I had awoken in the middle of a dream.

I glanced over at the long awning where all the other tenants parked. Still no Black Dodge or red Toyota.

"Shit!" I decided to find myself something for supper. Tossed a macaroni and cheese TV dinner in the microwave and poured myself a glass of iced tea and ate in silence at my little table.

I took my time about eating. Wasn't any reason to hurry. I thought about how much my life had changed with no hubby or father to order me around and make my life miserable, but that had nothing to do with my dedicating to Father Satan. I thoroughly enjoyed my freedom, that was indisputable, but I was lonely. Really lonely. Especially when I wasn't working.

Erick came to mind. I hadn't seen him in forever, it seemed. Maybe I'd take a walk in the park. Dark was just settling in, but I didn't much care. At that time, nothing seemed to matter much. What's more, most of the times I had come across him had been after dark.

I put my empty plastic plate in the garbage can under the sink, brushed my teeth, and decided to take that walk. It was still very warm out, had been in the nineties all day, and being out in the night air was still a relief from the day's hot sunshine. There was something going on at Dad's church. I saw a bunch of folding chairs sat up – revival! Dad loved to have revivals outdoors on the church lawn.

I thought I saw Greg running around like a chicken with his head cut off, doing his best to get everything ready. I couldn't help but wonder if he appreciated me more now that I wasn't there to do all the endless menial jobs for him and my father. I figured he would be much too busy to notice anything going on around other than focusing on the service, so I decided to sit down on one of the park benches facing towards the church. It was just far enough from the streetlight that he might not be able to make out who I was, should he look my way. Besides, I had the feeling he had given up on me. After all, he very well knew where I worked and so did my dad. Neither of them had come in the library to look for me when I was there or when I wasn't. Mrs. Peters would have told me right away if they had.

Service had started a little late, but Dad always held them late when outside, waited until it cooled off so the parishioners wouldn't be uncomfortable. There is something about the night air after a hot day. It is so refreshing. What's more, the church often picked up new members when revivals were held, especially when outside. More people notice that something is going on when they pass by. I suppose that is the purpose of such activities. It seems to work.

I think I sat there for a good half hour. Greg had led the congregation in a prayer and a couple of hymns, and then Dad got up to preach. Just hearing him harp on and on about love and forgiveness, knowing that he didn't understand a word he was trying to convey to the others simply nauseated me. I had had enough and got up to walk away. I wasn't sure where I was going. I just wasn't ready to go home yet.

The sidewalk framed the entire park, so I decided to take the long way around to my apartment, which would be about four blocks. It would be a good little walk, and I thought that perhaps by then I would be ready to return home. Maybe there would be something on the television now that I wanted to watch. I sure hoped so. Even if Nancy and Paul were home by now, I wasn't sure I should bother them this late. They had been gone ever since I got home from work earlier. I thought maybe she was working late at Baskin Robbins and maybe he was out with some of his buddies. Either way, I figured they wouldn't want company now. So I just began walking slowly towards my apartment, watching the cars pass as I went.

There was a tall shadow coming down the walk towards me. At first, I hoped it was Erick, but as he drew closer, I realized he had dark hair and it was short, not blonde and in a ponytail. My stomach sank. I really did want to see Erick. And I wondered why it was that we had never exchanged phone numbers or anything. My attention went back to the man. I couldn't see his face clearly, as the light was behind him now. He looked at me and smiled kind of strangely as he went by. I got really weird vibes from him. Made me uneasy. I sped up my walking pace, but I didn't want to let on that I was nervous. I had another block to go. I didn't dare look back either, afraid he might be watching me, and I didn't want him to know he had unnerved me. Suddenly, I heard someone running behind me – coming my way. I hoped, oh how I hoped, it was Erick. I dared to look.

It wasn't Erick. It was the dark-haired man! He was coming back.

I quickly snapped my head back around and continued walking, but I noticed the stranger hadn't passed me, but I could hear him behind me. He was walking now, not jogging. I did not like the feeling I was getting at all. I didn't know what else to do. I could no longer contain my composure; I took off running, heading across the park diagonally, cutting the distance as much as I could. To my horror, I realized the jogger had quickened his pace and was right behind me. *Oh god!* I knew then that coming to the park this time of night and not staying under the lights had been a bad idea. A very bad idea.

I ran faster, but the man was gaining on me. My side was hurting now, and I held it with my right hand, as I could hardly breathe. Then he grabbed my arm with a grasp of steel, and I just knew I was a goner, when, all of a sudden, a short figure – wearing a hoodie – dashed out from behind one of the big elm trees. I could just see him out of the corner of my right eye, as he quickly ran between me and my would-be attacker, tripping him. The man fell flat on his face.

"Hurry!" the little man said in an almost childlike voice that fit his stature.

I glanced at those twinkling eyes long enough to realize he was the same dwarf that had been in my room earlier. I was really puzzled, but he was obviously attempting to help me. Only, the man was so much bigger than he was. I didn't see how he could possibly stop him.

The jogger rose to his feet, but at once the little man leapt on his back and began pounding the jogger's head mercilessly with his fists. The man was yelling and frantically reaching back, trying to get the little guy off his back.

The dwarf saw that I was still looking, and he yelled at me again. "Don't just stand there! Hurry! Go home!"

I nodded yes and took off for my apartment. I could still hear the jogger shouting obscenities and begging for the dwarf to stop as I unlocked my door and ran in, locking it behind me. I leaned back against my door. "What in the world?" Who was he? Where had he come from? And he certainly was fully solid in the park. "Oh my God!"

I was simply blown away.

Trembling, I decided to take a shower, hoping it would still my nerves. I think I stayed in there for a good twenty minutes, but I finally came out. I went ahead and slipped into my shorty pajamas, as it was much too hot for anything else, and decided to have a glass of warm milk before going to bed. Watching television was out for now. I wasn't in the mood. I went in the kitchen, poured myself a tall glass of milk, sat down to the table, took a sip, and then realized the little man was standing in the doorway of my kitchen. "What on Earth?" I coughed, choking on my milk. "How did you get in?"

He avoided my question. "Just wanted to make sure you are okay, little lady. You are, aren't you?"

"Yes I am... Thank you!"

"I am pleased!" he smiled pleasantly, turned and disappeared into my living room.

I got up to see where he went – but he wasn't in the room. "Where did you go?" No answer. I hadn't heard the door open or close. And I was sure I locked it when I came in. Darn sure. I opened it anyway and looked out. No one in sight. "Huh?" This was really strange. I closed the door, secured the lock again and returned to my milk. I knew it was futile, but I searched for him some more after I finished my milk. Where had he gone? Things were just getting stranger and stranger. Then I remembered what Paul had said, "Expect the unexpected."

I knew I wouldn't go to sleep right away, so I picked up a novel I had checked out at the library. I would read until I grew tired. I think I must have fallen asleep around three. Of course, the light was still on when I awoke at eight the next morning.

Although the library was open Sunday afternoons, I was off. So I had another day to try and figure out what I was going to do with my time.

I spent the morning cleaning up my little apartment: mopped the kitchen floor, ran my little vacuum cleaner I had picked up at Wal-Mart, over the carpet in the living room and my bedroom. Straightened up my closet and was just about ready to make myself a sandwich when there was a knock on my door. I was delighted to see it was Nancy and Paul. Eagerly, I invited them inside and offered them a cold Coke, which they accepted. We then sat down in the living room.

"I'm so glad you came by," I said. "I was off yesterday as well, but neither of you were home. I was bored to tears."

"I had to work a double shift at Baskin Robbins," Nancy replied. "But I'm happy to know I was missed." She grinned.

Paul spoke, "I took the day off from work here and went in to help Nancy. Mike Lee caught a flu bug or something. And it being exceptionally hot, they were overrun with customers. Consequently, Nancy really needed help. So she called me and asked me if I could come in. I decided what the hey – A few extra greens in the wallet never hurt a body."

"I was wondering…" The little dwarf had been on my mind all day. I wasn't really certain who or even what he was. But he had sure come to my rescue.

"What's the funny look for?" Paul inquired, observing me intently.

"I'm not really sure how to bring this up."

Paul sat his can of Coke on the coffee table and leaned forward. "You can tell us anything, Brenda. You know that, don't you?"

"Ah… Not sure how to address this."

"Go ahead. Try us," Nancy encouraged.

"Know anything about dwarves?"

They shared a grin and then turned to me. "Why? Have you seen one?" Paul said.

I bobbed my head yes.

"You must have gone through with the dedication." Nancy remarked.

"Yes I did."

"I wasn't sure you had," Paul said. "You indicated that you were going to when we spoke about it, but you didn't ask for any tools."

"I went ahead and ordered them online. They came in three days. Must have forgotten to mention it."

"Good! That's cool."

"So, go ahead and fill us in about this dwarf," Nancy said, looking all curious and amused.

I told them the best I could exactly when I had seen him first, and how he hadn't appeared solid the first time, but when he rescued me in the park, and later, in my apartment, he appeared solid as anyone.

I swear Paul was grinning so big one would have thought he'd won a big prize. "Freakin' awesome!"

"Well," I inquired with a shrug, "can you tell me anything? Have you seen him?"

"We've seen dwarves. Not necessarily your dwarf."

"Did the ones you've seen wear hoodies?"

Paul chuckled. "Yes. They all wear them. Don't ask me why. They just do."

"I've never seen any of them without a hoodie either," Nancy confirmed.

"What can you tell me about them?"

"From what I understand, I believe they come out of Egypt, but before that, not sure."

Nancy took a sip of her soda and said, "Many of them are guardians. Also, I believe the Hopi Indians speak of them. I know they were mentioned on an episode of *Ancient Aliens* once."

Paul nodded in agreement. "I see them every now and then. They are guardians, but they are also quite playful."

"How's that?"

"Mischievous. They like to tease… play games with you. Hide things from you. And you can tear the room apart… or your car… and not find what you are looking for. Then, a few days later… sometimes weeks later, whatever you were looking for will often be just where you left it out in plain sight. Either that or some place you would never dream of finding it."

"Okay. Thanks for warning me."

Paul finished off his Coke and went to throw the can away in the garbage, but I told him not to worry about it. He nodded and said, "And there's one more thing. Don't let their size fool you. Those little guys are powerful! I do believe they could pulverize any prize fighter our world has to offer."

"Seriously?" I asked, remembering the man in the park screaming while the dwarf pounded his head mercilessly.

"Seriously," Nancy agreed. "Clifford, a friend of ours swears one lifted his Chevy truck off of him when the jack slipped. Saved his life. What's more, he said the dwarf hardly appeared winded. Soon as he saw to it that Clifford was okay, he just vanished."

"Wow!"

"But they only protect those of us who are dedicated to Father Satan," Paul said, emphasizing with a raised brow.

"That is so wild! I would have never dreamed such a thing possible. Shit! I didn't even know these little dwarves existed. Let alone, are our protectors."

"That's only part of it," Nancy said, eyes afire with enthusiasm now.

Paul agreed, "Yes… There is much, much more. You will ask yourself over and over how in the world did the world get so screwed up. Why people are told such lies and made to fear the very God that really and truly loves us? But, that is the way it is. It is our job to see to it that we can get the truth out to as many folks as we can. We need to do this for Father."

"I totally agree," I anxiously replied. "I am just blown away."

"Prepare to be blown away even more. I am sure that is not all you are going to see."

"Wow!" I shook my head. Already, I was beside myself. It was all so new and so very fascinating.

"Have you begun your meditations yet? They are essential in your Kundalini rising."

I was embarrassed to admit, "Not really. I know you mentioned something about it before and there is a great deal of information about it on a number of websites. But I'm not really totally clear on what it is."

The couple in front of me shared a mutual grin. Then Paul went on to explain, "All of us have the ability to raise our Kundalini. The meaning comes from Sanskrit, and stems from the yogic philosophy. It is corporeal energy known as 'shakti'. It is spiritual indwelling energy that is there for each one of us to be awakened."

"Oh?"

"Once awakening has been achieved, with consistent meditation, it can result in a raised Kundalini, which is enlightenment and complete bliss." He sat back and laid an arm around Nancy's shoulder, but continued, "It is a libidinal, unconscious force."

"Wow!"

Nancy interjected, "I'm kind of surprised that you were able to see your dwarf. Your third eye must already be partially opened. Otherwise, not sure you would have seen him."

Paul nodded in agreement. "Nancy's right... Are you psychic in any way?"

"You mean like knowing things before they happen? Dreams and such?"

"Yes."

"I sometimes know when the phone is going to ring... Or when a letter is coming. Things like that. Dad, of course, always said it was of the devil. Had a fit if I even mentioned any of those things."

"Not surprised. He is spiritually cut off. As long as he has that kind of blind attitude, he will never be able to know true spiritual enlightenment."

Nancy added, "Unfortunately, that is the way most Jews, Christians, Muslims and even some of whom are Hindu are. Depends. It's not really their fault though. They simply believe what they've always been taught and don't know any better. But to quote the X-files, 'The truth is out there'."

Paul grinned approvingly at Nancy and turned back to me. "What she says is true. Still, there's a good possibility that you were chosen by Father Satan. In which case, He's been with you all along. You just didn't know it."

"Seriously?"

"Seriously. And…while we're at it, the serpent in the Garden of Eden is none other than the representative of the Kundalini! Not a real serpent. But the gods were at war with one another. Anu, the father of Enki and Enlil wanted to keep mankind as slaves. He didn't want man to grow and learn, and to become like the gods. But, Enki did! Enki loves us! He has fought for us all along. That is the true tree of knowledge. The Kundalini is often depicted as two serpents entwined around the spine – Sound familiar?"

"You mean the symbol for doctors or the medical field. Those serpents?"

"Exactly! That's where it came from."

"Whew! I would have never guessed any of this."

"Don't feel left out. Unfortunately, most of the world has been under the big lie for hundreds, actually thousands, of years."

"This is huge!" I said. It was almost overwhelming to assimilate.

Paul glanced at Nancy and returned his attention back to me. "And there's something else."

"More?" I asked, already astounded.

Nancy bobbed her head yes, apparently knowing what Paul was getting at.

"Demons," Paul said.

"Demons? Yeah. I've been kind of expecting to see them… Something. Actually, still have some of that fear left over."

"It takes a while," Paul said. "But you need to know that they aren't the ugly, misshapen, hideous creatures that Christianity, Judaism, and the Islamic nation would have us believe." He grinned. "You have your dwarf."

"Oh?"

"He's not unpleasant to look at, is he?"

"No. Not at all. He's just a cute dwarf."

"Think about it. In the Bible, what are demons referred to as being? Fallen angels, right?"

I nodded yes.

"They're *not* fallen though. If you dig a little deeper, the term fallen actually is a roundabout reference to ones fallen Kundalini. Only the demons do not have fallen Kundalinis. However, I suggest that you need to read *The Epic of Gilgamesh* to begin with."

"I did read it. And it was quite an eye-opener. However, I wasn't certain how much is true."

"Why don't you read it again?"

"Okay. I will."

"But seriously, you do need to meditate, not only to raise your Kundalini serpent, but so you can handle the energies of your demon friends."

"Seems like I heard that before, but I don't fully understand." I shrugged. "The dwarf didn't bother me?."

"You weren't that physically close to him. Nor were you close to him long enough."

"Oh!"

Nancy sat forward. "Believe me, Brenda. You will understand what we mean when you do have a close encounter with one."

"Okay...Want to elaborate?"

"Here's how I see it." He glanced at Nancy, smiling wryly, and then turned back to me. "Nancy doesn't agree with me on this one. She seems to think they are different. However, from what I have read and studied, I believe that Demons and angels are the same species, if you can call them a species? They are still every bit as beautiful as they were in the beginning, before this war between Anu's followers and Enki's. Let's put it this way: It's like the difference between the Democrats and Republicans… and more extremely… between a democracy and a totalitarian state. When it comes right down to it – it is political! Political on a supernatural scale!"

Nancy interjected, "I agree on the political thing. Just not their species being the same. I think angels are the gray aliens."

He winked affectionately at her. "It's okay, babe. There are plenty of Spiritual Satanists out there who believe the way you do. And though I agree with them on most everything else, I still say angels and demons are the same species. However, there are gray aliens working with their side. I know, I've seen them enough times."

Jennifer let out a short laugh and smiled. She wasn't going to push their minor disagreement. Paul obviously understood and gave her a big hug.

"Okay, "I replied. "See if I understand what you are saying correctly. The Jews, Christians, and Muslims are all followers of Anu. But true Satanists are followers of Enki?"

"Exactly! However, do not confuse LeVayans with us. They actually do not believe in Father as a real being. They are atheist and just want to live an unbridled life. Live for whatever makes them happy; which, in a way, is their right and their choice. However, they aren't doing Father any favors in using His name. They are not spiritual at all. Then, there are the sickos who want to make blood, animal, or worse, sacrifices. Many of these people are just pure evil and have nothing to do with true Satanism at all. They just use Father's name to justify their hideous, fiendish acts, which does not help Father at all. Of course, His true name is Ea-Enki. And He has been called many names: Lucifer, Chemosh, and others. However, we prefer to call Him Father Satan or Father Enki."

Nancy leaned her head on Paul's shoulder. "Yes… Enki doesn't turn as many heads as Satan does. Most folks don't even have a clue as to who Enki is."

"I have to confess that I didn't either."

"Back to the energies. You obviously have a dwarf to watch over you, a guardian. You will probably have other guardians too, and not necessarily another dwarf or dwarves. You will come in contact with other demons as well. Father will probably assign you one, if he hasn't already. Could very well be the dwarf? Thing is, their bio-electricity is much higher and stronger than ours. Therefore you *must* raise your own energy in order to handle being around them. Their auras could attach to yours. And if your energy isn't high enough, it can be a little unpleasant."

"Oh? How?" I inquired, rubbing my right forearm just at the suggestion.

"Like a thousand mosquitoes biting all over your body," Nancy replied.

"Oh my God! I can't stand mosquitoes biting me."

"Well," Paul said, eyeing his girlfriend and then turning back to me "it has a lot to do with how personal the relationship is. It's not always that intense." He grinned wryly. "Depends on just how close one gets to a particular demon."

"Still," Nancy said, "About drove me nuts at first."

"I know, babe. But it didn't last long."

"True."

I had a feeling they were speaking about something I didn't quite understand, but I didn't push the issue. I spoke then, "I have begun meditating some, at least once, sometimes twice, a day. Took a couple of weeks but I feel I'm slowly getting it awakened."

"Good! You need to meditate every day, if possible," Paul said to me and removed his arm from around Nancy's shoulder and sat forward and reached in his pocket. He handed over a couple of sheets of folded paper. "Here. I copied down some energy-boosting meditations for you."

I gladly accepted them. "Thanks."

"And contrary to popular belief, you will find that Father's demons are the warmest, friendliest, and most considerate and loving beings you could ever come across. They are highly respectful of us. And they deserve the same. Threat them with utmost respect. And never… ever show fear to them! That is one of the biggest insults you could ever place upon a demon."

"Wow! I am so glad you told me."

"However, I am sure they understand a new member to Father's family as being a little anxious. You'll soon learn though just how wonderful they truly are."

"And just wait until Father hugs you!" Nancy said, smiling hugely. "His hugs are the most wonderful of feelings you could ever possibly experience!"

"Seriously?"

"She's right about that. You will feel the greatest love and warmth you will ever know. It is beyond description. Let us know when you get a hug."

"Oh! Yes! I will definitely do that," I said with anticipation. "I can't wait!"

Paul glanced at his wristwatch. "Well, we have some running around we want to do. But we wanted to see how you've been doing."

"And I've been anxious to see you both too."

They stood and I followed them to the door. "Thanks for coming. It has been most enlightening."

"Keep up those meditations," Paul said.

Nancy added, "Come on by Baskin Robbins when you get a chance. I'll give you a free cone of coffee ice cream."

I smiled at that. "Thanks! You better believe I'll be there."

Paul gave me a shoulder-hug, and then Nancy hugged me. With nods, they left, and I closed my door.

I turned and stared into my living room. "Wow! Guess I have a lot to do."

I put away the empty cans and straightened up the living room a little. Then I unfolded the papers Paul gave me and sat down in the middle of the living room floor and, following Paul's instructions, began my first, serious meditation.

Chapter Eleven

I had been lucky for a few weeks without Dad or Greg noticing my car pulling in at my apartment. It was only a few blocks down from them, and had they been on the road or in Greg's yard and looking down towards the park, they could have seen my car from that distance. I figured it was only a matter of time, but I kept hoping, and so far, so good.

I was careful when I stepped outside my apartment when it was daylight. Always peeping out first to make sure I didn't see one of their cars going by or one of them in the yard. It wasn't the best of circumstances, but I was free. And that made the efforts at keeping a low profile worthwhile. Of course, both Greg and Dad knew where I worked.

The past week, though, Dad did come in the library a couple of times, but he never said so much as boo to me, if and when he did spot me. I could tell by his cold, cold eyes, that he was much too pissed at what *I had done* to them. He considered me a lost sinner, and therefore had no more reason to even talk to me. Funny thing was he didn't even have a clue that I had become a Satanist!

I'm sure with his twisted beliefs about Satanism he would figure, should he have found out, that that was the way I had always been headed – which would have been damnation by his opinion.

Of course, that was not what I was feeling at all. Never had I felt so good, so right, about everything. I was learning to meditate. I didn't feel like I was getting anywhere for a while, but it was becoming easier, and I was beginning to feel my energy rising. And that in itself was something I was quickly learning – the sensation, the feel of such wonderful energy surrounding my body. It was awesome!

When I ran into Paul one late afternoon at the park, I asked him about it, and he seemed really pleased with my progress. He did ask me if I had seen the dwarf anymore, and I admitted that I hadn't. He said that wasn't unusual. Sometimes they didn't seem to mind letting us see them, and then other times, we would hardly see them at all.

Still, they would leave their little calling cards, as Paul had previously warned me about. I would leave my keys on the kitchen counter, and when I'd go to get them, they wouldn't be there. Found them in my right sneaker once, and another time, I found them on top of my pillow.

One evening I was getting ready to cook a TV dinner in my microwave, and I set it inside and hit the five minute button and walked off towards the bathroom, heard a beep, and knew it had been much too soon, not even a full minute. I swirled around on my heels and went back. It had been turned off. So, I hit the five minute button again, and this time I actually made it to the bathroom before I heard the beep. "You little stinker!"

I marched right back to the kitchen. Off again. "Will you please let my dinner cook?" I said, scanning my surroundings, and I could swear that I heard soft snickering. I shook my head and once more touched the five minute button. Got to the bathroom this time and managed to pee. When I returned to the kitchen I saw that my dinner was indeed cooking – but it was set for thirty minutes! "Shit!" I couldn't help it. I laughed. Of course, I shut it off and reset it for two.

Knowing full well that the second I walked away he would mess with it again, I just stood there until it was done. I could still hear low giggling, almost like a child off in what sounded like the living room. I took a look, but of course he wasn't about to let me see him. "Oh well." My dinner was ready. I took it out, sat it on the table and went to fill myself a glass of ice from my little freezer at the top of my refrigerator, poured tea in, grabbed a fork out of the drawer and went back to the table.

No dinner.

"You little turd!" I squealed and walked into the living room. This time, it was outright laughter I heard. "Where is my dinner?" There was a scuffling of feet in the kitchen. I returned to find my dinner placed exactly where I had put it. "Thank you!" I said and sat down before he decided to put it somewhere else. I sat there shaking with muted laughter for several minutes. At least, he was letting me know he was still around. I didn't mind putting up with his shenanigans, for I knew he would protect me in a heartbeat. Besides, he did add a little laughter to sometimes otherwise boring days or evenings.

I didn't know his name though, and I wanted to know his name. So I just came right out and asked, "What's your name?" There was a long moment of silence and I was pretty sure he wasn't going to answer, and then I heard, "Cal. Call me Cal."

"Thank you, Cal." I thought about it a minute. "Would you like something to eat?" I wasn't sure if he ate the food we did. For it was obvious he was from a parallel realm. He could come into our world, but could he eat or even want to eat our food?

"It's okay," I heard his little voice reply. "Cal not hungry."

"Okay. Well, if you ever want anything I have, just say so. To eat, that is."

"Thanks but Cal okay."

"Yes, indeed, you are okay. Thanks for being here for me."

"It's what I do," he replied.

Then everything got really quiet and I had the distinct feeling he had left. "Cal?"

No response. He was gone. I went ahead and finished my dinner. I would take my shower, meditate for a while, watch a little television, and then retire to bed. Even though Cal wasn't there at that moment, somehow I knew he would be there in a flash if I needed him. It was a good feeling. No. It was a wonderful feeling.

*

I spent the next few weeks meditating as much as possible, when I wasn't at work, and then taking long walks in the park. A couple of times, I thought I saw Erick jogging along the far side by the parallel street, but then I would lose sight of him and that would be it. He never came around to my side. I even went out of my way once to turn and go towards where I thought he should be coming from, but I didn't meet up with him. In fact, I didn't see him at all then.

Did I want to see him so badly that I was imagining glimpses of him? Or was it something else? Was he more than human as I had suspected on several occasions? I'd shake my head then and tell myself that I was being silly – but then I remembered Cal. Cal was definitely no ordinary human. But he was real! Very real! So maybe Erick was of an otherworldly origin? Whatever he was, I missed his friendship.

Now that I had had time to settle in my apartment and work myself into somewhat of a normal routine, I realized that I was lonely… Very lonely. It hit me more when watching television. I found I couldn't watch romantic movies at all. I searched for comedies or documentaries and ended up watching a lot of shows on the History channel. And I definitely wasn't going to watch any religious shows. No way at all!

Even though I had no intentions of going back to Greg, I still kind of missed what we once had. Or, at least, what I thought we had. I missed being held and I missed being made love to. As much as I hated to admit it, I missed having a sexual relationship. I was a young woman with normal needs. But there was no way I was going to go back to Greg. Besides, the romance had gone out of our love-making some time ago. It was mostly his being satisfied and my being left high and dry and very frustrated. That was definitely not what I was looking for or what I needed.

I needed to feel loved and cherished, and wanted to love and cherish back. There was no way I could do that with a controlling, insensitive husband. But what was I to do? I didn't want to date yet. I wasn't divorced. In fact, to my knowledge, no divorce had been filed. I certainly hadn't sought one.

I'd been surfing through the channels and not finding anything I was interested in, I turned my television off. The time on the cable box said ten-thirty. I had to work the morning shift the next day, so I decided to just go take my shower and call it a night.

I went to my bedroom and stood in front of my dresser drawers, thinking to grab my light blue, shortie pajamas, when I suddenly had a warm sensation on both shoulders from behind. Not sure what it was, I thought perhaps I was imagining it. I went to open the drawer but the sensation grew stronger – felt like two strong hands resting on my shoulders. My heart skipped a beat. "What the heck?" Had someone broken into my apartment? I spun around. No one there... Or so I first thought. I stood there puzzled for only a moment and turned back to get my pajamas. "You're losing it, Brenda," I told myself. "Really losing it!" I grabbed my pajamas and went on to the bathroom and took my shower, doing my best not to think about what had happened.

Showered and ready for bed, I set my alarm for seven-thirty and then grabbed a glass of water from the kitchen and set it by my clock radio. I slipped into bed and turned out the light.

I have to admit, that I was a little uneasy, wondering if the sensation of hands on my shoulders had been supernatural, but I didn't want to address it. Paul and Nancy had told me not to ever show fear when dealing with the supernatural; that fear was the only thing to fear. So, I said it to myself several times and closed my eyes. I wanted only to sleep. I didn't want to think about anything.

I lay there for some time and finally fell into blessed sleep. Then, in the middle of the night, I sensed what I believed to be a strong arm around my waist, holding me lovingly. In my dreamy state I believed myself to be back in bed with Greg, and he had his arm wrapped around me. I automatically placed my hand on his and felt him snuggle closer to me.

My eyes popped open. I lay there frozen for several seconds before gasping, "Oh my God!"

I leapt out of bed and quickly turned my lamp on. No one there! My heart was racing at this point. "Shit! Oh shit!"

Then, clear as a bell in my head, I heard, "It's okay, Brenda. I will never hurt you."

"…What? Where are you?" I frantically scanned my surroundings. I saw no one!

"I sensed your loneliness and came," he said, speaking in a wonderful euphonic voice.

"I don't see you! Where are you?"

"I'm right here in front of you. Just relax and try to focus. You should be able to see something of me."

"…Ah… yeah." I blew out air and waited for my heart to slow down. Then I ever so carefully tried to focus on the air in front of me. "I don't see anything but my bed and the room," I confessed.

"Relax. Look at the air! Focus on the air!"

That sounded crazy to me, but I did what he said. I stood there doing my best to see something – anything – in the air. Then I saw a bluish-white flickering light forming a curved line only a couple of feet away from me. Then another luminous, curved line formed a little to the left, and again, one slightly to the right, and then many appeared, and they began to coalesque for me.

Suddenly, I could make out the image of a man! At least, he was shaped like a man, but he was bluish-white, see-through, and very tall. I guessed him to be well over six feet. His head was smooth and perfectly shaped. I did not get any impression of hair.

"Well?" he said. "You do see me now, don't you?"

I bobbed my head yes. "Sort of."

I do believe he chuckled then. "You're doing well. Most humans do not see us that well at first. You are very open to supernatural presence."

I think that was a compliment. I just muttered, "Uh-huh."

"I did not mean to frighten you. Only to comfort you."

"I appreciate that," I replied. I kept remembering all I had been told, and what I had read about being respectful to any supernatural beings, and they would be respectful to you. That is, if they were from Father Satan. I remembered then to ask, "Are you from Father Satan?"

He hesitated not, "Yes! You need not worry. I have come to comfort you. However, if you wish me to leave, I will."

That surprised me. "I…" I played my eyes over his very beautiful but otherworldly frame. His shape was perfect!

He asked me again, "Do you wish me to leave? For I will, if you are uncomfortable with my being here. Just say the word, Brenda. I will go."

"No! No! Don't go."

I think he smiled, but I couldn't tell exactly. I just sensed it. "Good. For I like you and I hope to be your friend."

The question had been in my head for several seconds, but I had not asked.

He knew, though. "Yes! I am a demon."

"But you're pretty!" I blurted, not thinking.

I know he smiled then. I could barely make out the edges of his mouth turning up at the corners. "Thank you!" There was a low chuckle.

"Nancy and Paul told me that demons weren't ugly… that that was just a bunch of bull shit."

"So, now you know," he said, now with a smile in his voice.

He sat down on the bed and patted it with his hand. "Sit down with me."

So I did.

"Anything you want to know about me, just ask."

"Well, you are a demon, but there's this dwarf by the name of Cal. He saved me from being attacked in the park one night, but he's very mischievous."

"Yes. The little guys are very playful."

"He's a demon too?"

"Yes. We come in a number of varieties," he said.

"What…What kind of demon are you?"

"I knew you were going to ask. Well, I am a couple of things. I am a soldier. I spend a lot of time fighting in the ongoing spiritual war that has raged practically since the beginning of time… and," he said, holding my gaze, "I'm also an incubus."

That I really had not even considered, but I don't know why. "Oh?" I said with great surprise, and my mouth must have dropped open, for he reached up with his forefinger and pushed my chin up, closing my mouth.

"You're surprised?"

I nodded yes. "I suppose I am."

"Again, expected something a bit more homely?"

"I'm sorry."

"Don't be. It takes a while to get over all the brainwashing."

"So… Ah… Not sure how to ask this—."

"You want to know if I came to have sex with you?"

"I guess that's what I wanted to ask."

"Only if you want to, Brenda. It is your choice. I sensed your loneliness, and I've been looking for a human female to have a relationship with. Not many of your kind who are open to my kind, especially with all the lies about us available."

"Yes. Considering all the crap people are taught… not only in Christianity but Judaism and Islam… I can see where there might not be many."

"It's not the only factor. I'm not human. Most women want a human mate. That narrows it down considerably more." He turned slightly more towards me. "When I sensed your loneliness and your… desire… I didn't waste a second in coming. For I desire a mate very much. But I am willing to merely be your friend, if you do not wish for a sexual relationship with me."

I could not help but wonder what that would be like. "Would it be monogamous? And would it be permanent?"

"If you wish to remain open to the possibility of a future human partner, I can be very open with that. As long as I understand that, there would not be a problem. Or if you wish to be with only me, then it will be with only me. And I would expect you to keep your promise on that. I would be faithful to you in the same respect."

"That's really cool," I replied, but I wasn't sure at that moment whether I wanted to have sex with him or not. I wouldn't want to have sex with a human man that I'd just met either. There were too many questions as yet to be answered.

Knowing my thoughts, he said, "Don't worry. I have no intentions of having sex with you until and unless you want it and are ready. I just want to be here for you to comfort you for now. I am here to be your friend."

I stared into what I could now clearly see were brilliant, indigo eyes that danced with little sparkles. Though his face was bluish-white, I could now see his body pretty visibly. It looked to me as though he was wearing some kind of amour. For some reason, a King Arthur Knight came to my mind. Although I know that wasn't the case. "You're really very sweet."

"I try to be." He seemed pleased that I said that.

I suddenly realized that I was tingly all over, even itching in spots. I scratched the fold of my left arm.

He smiled.

"What?" I asked, staring up at him inquisitively.

"My energy is getting to you."

"Oh! Is that what it is? Itches!" It was growing more intense by the second.

"Sorry about that. Demons have that effect on humans, especially when we are close."

Now I was really itching. "Is there anything I can do?"

"For the moment, go take a hot shower. As hot as you can stand it. It will help regulate your body's energy with mine. Then put lotion all over your body. I understand that helps with the itching too. But tomorrow when you meditate, concentrate on power meditations to not only raise but also to boost your energy. Otherwise, it will be rough on you when you are close to demons. Especially me, if we make love."

"Cal didn't affect me this way."

"You weren't this close to him, were you?"

"No," I replied.

"Besides, chances are, he will never get as close to you as I am."

"Okay!" I jumped up, now scratching wildly.

"Tell you what. I'll leave for now. But I'll be back in a few days after you do some power meditations to raise your energy. But if you need me for any reason, any reason at all, just think real hard and I will come."

"Okay… But what is your name?"

"Paleo. Just call me Paleo."

"Okay. Is that your real name? Or a nickname?" I considered my question for a second, and then asked, "Do demons have nicknames."

"Sometimes. For humans, anyway. Paleo is my 'nickname'. I doubt if you could pronounce my real name," he said and then vanished.

I was clawing at myself now and couldn't wait to get in the hot shower. And he was right. When I stepped out, I felt much better. I remembered the lotion too and applied that quickly. There was still some residual energy, but I was able to stand it and went right to sleep.

*

All during the following week, I did my best to be faithful in my meditations, and building my aura and energy. I couldn't help but think of Paleo. He was so different from anyone I could have ever imagined. Then I had to question myself: Had I imagined him? Was I finally really losing it? I hadn't said a word to Nancy and Paul about him. After all, having an incubus for a friend was kind of personal. Of course, I hadn't had sex with him. I have to admit, though, that I was growing more and more curious about what a relationship with him would be like.

Did I really want to have a sexual relationship with a demon? There had been a time when such a thought would have horrified me, but not since I had actually met an incubus. He had given me no reason whatsoever to fear him. On the contrary, I had felt strangely safe in his presence.

I finally had a day off. It happened to be a Saturday. It didn't take me long to clean up my apartment, for it didn't get very messy, as I was somewhat of a neat-freak. Done with my menial chores, I decided that I would walk down and see if Nancy or Paul was home. Just as I went to open my door I heard a small but familiar voice behind me. "You like him, don't you?"

I spun around. "Cal! Haven't seen you in a while."

He smiled confidently. "Oh... I've been around."

"I bet you have."

"But you do like him, don't you?"

"Who?"

"You know... You like Paleo... the incubus. Curiosity getting the better of you?"

"Cal! That's kind of personal. He seems nice. But I'm not sure I want an intimate relationship with him."

"Hmmm," he mused. Then he got a really big grin on his face. "Still, you like him."

"Yes! From what little I know of him. He seems really polite."

"Oh, he's much more than that."

Then it hit me. "You wouldn't be here on his behalf, would you?"

"Of course not," he briskly replied.

I tilted my head curiously. "Cal... "

He wrinkled his nose in a most charming way. "Can't say." Poof! He was gone.

"Okay," I said to myself. I stood there momentarily, and I couldn't help but smiling. It seemed that demon males might not be so different from human ones at that. I opened the door and headed on down to Nancy's and Paul's.

Neither Paul nor Nancy was home, so I decided to take a walk in the park. I did notice a lot of cars at my father's church and wondered what was going on. After all, it was Saturday. I walked on down and sat on one of the benches that was under a shade tree. I was getting to the point that I didn't care if anyone saw me or not.

I was free of them now and no longer afraid of them. I had a job, my own place, and good friends, human and supernatural.

After a little bit, a group of folks came rushing out of the church and stood in lines on each side of the walk. Then a couple dressed in white came out – a wedding!

There was a lot of laughter and rice being thrown about as the couple ran down the steps, sidewalk, and to a red Mazda that I just realized had 'just married' painted in big white letters on the back. Someone had tied a few cans to the rear bumper.

I was there for about five minutes when I noticed a jogger coming down the walk from my right. I couldn't believe it – Erick! He smiled broadly and came over and plopped down beside me.

"I was beginning to think I wasn't ever going to see you again," I said.

Still smiling, he replied, "I've been around, Brenda."

"Funny. Everyone seems to say that."

"Oh?"

"It's nothing."

He furrowed his brow curiously. "You sure?"

I screwed up my mouth, eyeing him intently. Then I finally got the guts to say it, "Are you—?"

"Am I what?"

I blew out air. "There are times when I get the feeling that you are different."

"In what respect?"

"Honestly?"

"Yes. Please."

"Are you... human?"

He tilted his head back, eyeing me as though I had lost my mind. "What?"

I felt utterly ridiculous. "I... I'm sorry." I was at a loss for words knowing he must think me totally crazy. "That didn't come out right."

"Why on Earth would you think that I was anything else?"

I shrugged. How did I get out of this one? "I didn't literally think you weren't human," I lied, not wanting to admit what I had been thinking. "It just came out wrong. I meant it more in a teasing way."

"Oh!" He bobbed his head and grinned amusedly.

"It's just that in the past you have shown up just when I really needed someone. Kind of like you're a guardian angel of some kind. That's all. Yes. That's what I meant. You have this uncanny knack for being there for me when I need you. But I haven't a clue who you really are."

"I see. Makes sense." He leaned back, resting against the bench. "I live a couple of blocks from here... Opposite end of the park." He pointed to our left. I can just see your dad's church from my front porch. I live in a two story house... by myself. No family."

"Oh! So you're all alone?" I wondered about any family he might have, but I felt so foolish already I didn't bother to ask.

"Yes. But I'm used to it."

"That's good." I said, doing my best to appear somewhat normal, but I felt so silly it wasn't funny.

"It's okay, Brenda. You're right. I suppose it would seem really strange to you... the way we've come across one another several times and all."

"Yeah," I nodded. "But I am very grateful for all you've done for me. You have been absolutely awesome."

"Thank you." He stood then. "Well, I should get going." He glanced at his watch and then looked back at me. "No dilemmas this time?"

"No. Thank goodness!"

"Good to know. And good to see you again." He winked, and took off jogging again.

I'm not exactly sure why, but my heart kind of sank right then and there. I had actually let myself believe that Erick was kind of a guardian angel... or demon, depending on one's perspective. I definitely felt disappointment. Though he was a wonderful person, and I would be eternally grateful for all he had done for me, I was emotionally devastated – He was human. Albeit, a good one, but still, only human. I stood. "What in the world is wrong with me?" I decided to run too. I wasn't in jogging clothes, but I ran anyway, in the opposite direction, all the way back to my apartment.

*

A big shipment of books arrived on Saturday while I was off, but Miranda had managed to get only about half of them recorded in the computer and put away. Therefore, I had plenty to do on Sunday when the library opened up for the afternoon. I was kind of grateful. I had something to take my mind off of everything. I didn't want to think about any of the crazy events my life had taken a turn to in the past few months. Work was what I needed.

My disappointment in learning that Erick was simply an ordinary man had really bummed me out. I know it shouldn't have, but it did. I kept telling myself that I was being utterly stupid and silly, but it still didn't change the way I felt.

Miranda had been checking out all the patrons, but we got kind of busy around three, so I had to set aside the books I was filing in and help her get the crowd out. I had just finished checking out a young black woman and turned aside to take a drink of my bottled water, but when I looked back up I almost fell off my seat. "Mother!"

"Hello, Brenda," she said, eyes all misty and happy.

I was pretty much speechless. "You're really here?" I finally said in a noticeably cracked voice.

Looking lovingly apologetic, she replied, "Yes! I'm back, Brenda. I have been so worried about you. I couldn't take it any longer. I had to see you. I couldn't believe it when your father told me that you and Greg had married, but you had left Greg and moved out… Are you okay?"

I couldn't help it. I started laughing. Laughing at the absurdity of it all.

Miranda looked at me strangely.

I shook my head. "I'm sorry," I said to my boss, managing to stifle my laughter, "But this is my mother."

"Oh?" she replied with a puzzled frown. But then looked away.

I turned back to my mother. "Now? Now you are concerned about me?"

Hurt flickered in her eyes, but she maintained a straight face. "I know I deserved that. But I did beg you to go to school."

Wriggling my head yes, I replied, "You did. I know you did. And it didn't take very long after Greg and I married for me to see what you'd been trying to tell me all along. I guess I can't blame you for leaving the way you did."

"Well, I shouldn't have left you, Brenda. But your dad is another story. I should have left his ass a long, long time ago." She glanced over at Miranda and then back to me. "What time do you get off?"

"Five," I replied, looking at my watch.

"You drive or walk?"

"Walked."

"How about I pick you up at five and we can eat at one of the little restaurants on the Riverwalk? Then we could go to your place or mine and visit for a while?"

"Sounds good, Mom. I had been just thinking of heating up a microwave dinner, but I am getting kind of tired of them."

"See you then. I'll let you get back to work."

"Okay, Mom." I smiled, and she gave my hand an affectionate pat and walked out.

Sure enough, Mom was waiting for me when I came out, leaning across the front seat and opening the door for me. I hopped in.

"You need to stop at your apartment for anything first?"

"Nope. I'm good. And so glad you're back. It's been really lonely without you."

"Been kind of lonely for me too, hon."

"Are you here for good now?" I was hesitant to ask, but I still had to know.

"As long as you need me, Brenda."

"You have a place to stay?"

"Yes! I rented a small apartment about a mile down the road from the park. Your dad said he thought you lived close. He's seen you in the park a lot, from what he says."

"Yes. I live in an apartment on the opposite end of the park from the church."

"You happy there?"

"I'm not being tormented and run to death by Dad and Greg."

Mom laughed at that. "Got ya."

"How are the two pastors?"

"They're pastors."

Now I was the one laughing.

"Greg misses you though. He really isn't quite as bad as your dad. But close. Give it a few more years and he will probably be just as bad."

"That's what scares me, Mom. I've seen him slowly growing more and more like Dad."

"It would take something short of a miracle to keep it from ruining him, I'm afraid. I've seen it happen too many times." She smiled over at me. "You know... We've seen numerous pastors and their families over the years. Only a handful of them seem to remain actually happy. The wives grow old, weary and frigid, and the kids rebel and run off. Often becoming delinquents in rebellion. Fortunately, not all of them. Some actually turn out okay."

"But not many," I said.

"I think if a pastor can truly keep his perspectives right, that he can do a lot of good and have a happy family too. Unfortunately, so many of them get a God complex. Like your dad. And now poor Greg seems to be headed down that same road."

"I know. I can see it."

It took some searching, but we finally found a place to park where we didn't have to walk too far. "Enough talk about them. Let's go get us something good to eat."

"Yeah." I agreed with a nod and got out. I glanced over at the folks in one of the riverboats gliding along the water by the Riverwalk. They all looked so happy. Dad had taken Mom and me there several times when I was a young girl, but that had been a few years ago.

Mom knew what I was thinking. She gave me a warm smile and said, "Been a while, hasn't it?"

"Yeah. It has."

"Maybe we'll ride it after we eat. Want to?"

That idea sounded good. "Sure. I'd love to."

"We'll do it then."

We went on to a little Italian restaurant then and chose one of the tables outside.

It was great having my mom around again. We spent a lot of time together the first week. She'd come over after I got off work, or I would go to her place. She had a new job as a receptionist for some local doctor, but hadn't started yet. The girl that she was to replace had another week. I even introduced her to Paul and Nancy. I could tell she wasn't real keen on them at first, but she was pleasant and not rude. She just thought them kind of 'hippy', but added that they were my friends, so she would respect that. Then one Friday night, they invited me and Mom over for pizza. She was cool with it, and we both had a good time. Paul was good at telling jokes and had us all entertained. We left with our sides hurting from laughing so much.

When we left, she let me know that she liked them better than at first sight. Still, there was something about them that was different. "They aren't church folk, are they?" she finally asked me.

"Not at all, Mom."

"I thought so. They are too relaxed and not uptight. I didn't see that false sweetness about them."

I had expected a different kind of comment, and thought it great that she said that. "False sweetness, huh? So you do like them a little?"

"Yes. I do. But I still pick up really different vibes. Can't put my finger on it, though."

"They're just not church folks," I reminded her.

"Yes. You're right. Maybe that's all it is."

Even though Mom had left church and Dad, I feared she would still have too much Christianity ingrained in her to understand me having Satanists friends, and even more so that I was a Satanist. Nope. As understanding and open-minded as she was, I had a feeling that she would not be that open. I would do my best to keep it to myself. I didn't have to tell Nancy and Paul either. They had been the ones that were adamant about keeping it quiet.

Chapter Twelve

With Mom back, I didn't feel so alone in the physical world anymore. I still spent as much time with Nancy and Paul that I could.

Mom came over most evenings when I worked the day shift. Then she would leave around nine, as she had to get up early weekdays for work. If Nancy and Paul were home, then I would go over to visit with them, especially on Mondays.

Monday is Satan's day of the week, and we often did a little ritual for Father Satan to honor Him. Then we'd give thanks for all He had done and was doing for us. We especially appreciated Him at this time, knowing how busy He had to be with so much war and conflict going on in the world.

I was amazed that He had time for us at all. For every now and then, I would hear His wonderful voice clear as a bell in my head, answering a question I had.

Awesome wasn't the word for Him. He is a true and loving God, one that actually answers prayers and questions no matter how busy. I cannot begin to express how much I had grown to love Him. It amazed me. What's more, as awesome and hard to believe as it was, I loved Father more and more daily. One has to truly know Him to understand the intensity of His love for us and ours for Him. There is no way an outsider can comprehend this.

All the hate and fear and lies that have existed for centuries were just that – lies! Such injustice to such a sweet, loving and caring God! Yet, He chooses not to retaliate. He simply strives to get the truth out there, and hopes that as many souls as possible can be saved from the ugly lies and mental slavery that has gone on for far too long.

I had not 'felt' or heard anything from the incubus. I thought that perhaps he had moved on and found another human female. I hadn't seen much of Cal either, but once in a while I would find something of mine in a strange place, where I knew there was no way I had put it there. One evening – it was a good thing I looked

– just as I went to pee, I noticed my car keys sitting in the bottom of the toilet. I spun around, "Cal!"

Distinct giggling came from my bedroom.

"You little turkey!" I immediately fished out my keys and ran the hot water over them for a good ten minutes, and washed both my hands and keys with soap. By the time I was done, it was all I could do not to wet myself before I sat down to finally pee.

Relief at last, I went on into the kitchen, halfway expecting Cal to be gone, but he wasn't. To my surprise, he was sitting at my little table spooning lots of sugar into a cup of coffee. It was fresh. I had just made it. He rolled his sparkling, bluish-gray eyes up to mine as if daring me to question his actions.

I didn't even consider scolding him, though. I knew he was there for me. It was just his nature to have a little fun. I felt it was too bad that more humans weren't like him. "I don't mind if you have a cup," I said and took an empty cup out of the cabinet and poured myself some. But when I sat down, he was still spooning sugar into his cup. I frowned. "What on Earth? I think you have more than enough sugar, Cal."

He merely chuckled, delighted that I thought so and stared, unblinking at me, while he spooned in another heaping spoonful.

"Oh my God! You will be sick!"

With his mischievous eyes fixed on mine, he spooned in one more.

I couldn't help it. I snatched up the sugar bowl. "Enough!"

He just laughed and took a sip of the now very thick coffee, still eyeing me daringly all the while.

I thought surely he would take a sip or two and discard it, but he didn't. He gulped down the whole cup. I think my jaw dropped about a foot. "You actually finished it?"

"Cal likes sugar," he said. "Thanks for the coffee!" He stood from his seat, set his cup in the sink, bowed graciously with a pleasant smile and vanished.

"Oh boy…" I wasn't sure what to think. "Okay. Glad you enjoyed it," I called out.

"I did!" was his response. There was a light laugh and then silence.

I sensed he was gone then.

The silence of the room was broken by a strong knock on my door. I wasn't expecting anyone. I knew Nancy was at work and Paul was helping her. Mom had left early, as she wanted to go home and work on her bills. So, I was hesitant to answer.

Whoever it was knocked again. I pulled my white curtain back and peeped out – Greg!

He had learned where I lived!

He knocked again. I seriously thought of not answering, but then decided I might as well face him. Obviously, he knew where I lived now. I opened the door a crack, but kept the chain lock in place. "What do you want?"

"To talk."

His face was stoic and hard to read. "There's nothing for us to talk about."

"We need to talk about our marriage."

"We don't have one," I coldly replied.

"Brenda, please let me in?"

I blew out air. "Okay… But I am in no mood to argue with you."

"I just want to talk. I won't be long."

I unlocked the chain and let him in. He looked around briefly. "Not bad for a small apartment."

"Thanks." I sat down on my little sofa but gestured for him to sit on the second-hand easy chair I had picked up from a neighbor who had moved out recently.

He nodded okay and took a seat.

I stared at him. "So, how did you find out where I live?"

"I saw your mother's car pull in yesterday evening. I knew where her apartment was, so I figured it had to be you."

"You could have come to the library, you know."

"Not a place to discuss personal matters."

"True."

"Brenda, I want you back," he suddenly said with pleading eyes.

"Greg, a part of me will always care about you." He went to respond but I put up a hand. "Let me finish."

"Okay."

"We are not even on the same playing field anymore. It will never work. Even if you have changed a lot of your ways and thinking."

"What do you mean exactly?" He sat forward. "Explain it to me."

No way could I tell him I was a Satanist. Something he would never understand, let alone accept. "I just don't believe the way you do anymore."

"What?" His face contorted in confusion.

"To put it bluntly. I have lost all faith in your God. I don't care if I ever step foot in a church, synagogue or mosque ever again!"

His faced flushed instantly red and he stood. "What on Earth is wrong with you?"

"Traditional religion and dictatorial pastors are what are wrong with me, Greg!"

He was aghast. "You don't mean that, Brenda."

"Never been more serious. What's more, I didn't invite you here. And since you can't hear the truth without getting all bent out of shape, it is time for you to leave."

He shut his eyes briefly, and I could tell he was trying to calm himself. When he opened his eyes again, he said, "You're right… About my coming without an invitation. But I can't believe you've completely lost your faith in God."

"Your God!" I said, realizing at the time I said it that way that it wasn't a good idea.

"Okay. What is this bit about 'your God'? Want to explain yourself?"

"I already told you. I don't have to explain myself to you or anyone else."

He stepped forward.

I could tell this could easily turn into an all-out fight. I lowered my voice. "You need to leave, Greg."

"Just explain to me what you mean. Do you mean Wicca?"

"Absolutely not! That's history now. And I don't have to explain anything. We don't live together anymore. I support myself. I have my own place. We don't share a bed anymore. What I do and what I believe is none of your damn business!"

"Expletives now?"

I didn't comment.

I could tell by his expression that he felt as though he'd been hit by a brick. "Then there is no discussing our marriage?"

"You just proved to me that that is impossible. Where did this conversation end up? Religion! And I take the blame for that. However, there is no way we will ever agree on our beliefs. Therefore, I am saying no! No hope for our marriage. It is already over. I just haven't bothered to file for divorce yet. Been busy working."

He twisted his tongue around as though pondering what to say. "So, that's it? You really want a divorce?"

I knew by his eyes that he wanted me to say no, but that wasn't going to happen.

"Yes! I have every intention of filing for divorce. We have irreconcilable issues."

His anger turned to sadness. I almost felt sorry for him but not quite. "Okay. I will file. I am sure I can afford it more than you can."

"But the church will only accept adultery as grounds for divorce, Greg. I haven't committed adultery. I don't want our divorce on a lie. Irreconcilable differences will be good enough for the courts."

"What am I supposed to tell the church?"

"Lie. Dad lied to the church. But I don't want a lie on public record. Hasn't he been excusing their divorcing on a lie? Mom hasn't committed adultery."

He thought it over momentarily and then nodded in agreement. "Okay. I guess if your dad can do it, then I can."

"Of course you can."

"All right." He let out a weary sigh and moved to the door.

I did get up and go to the door too.

With a very saddened countenance, he said, "I do still love you, Brenda. This I did not want."

"I'm sad too, Greg." And I was a little. I still cared a lot about him. "But it will never work."

Nodding in reluctant acceptance he made himself smile and went out. I closed the door behind him.

"Whew!" I breathed, glad that it was over.

Then I heard him yell and it sounded as though he fell to the ground. I swung the door back open. There was Greg sprawled out on the sidewalk rubbing the back of his head.

"What happened?"

He managed to pull himself up and stand to his feet. "Something gooey all over the walk here," he said, lifting his shoe for me to see the sole. Sure enough, something brownish and sticky looking slowly dripped to the walk. I recognized it right away – slightly regurgitated, sugary coffee.

Cal! You little shit!

I ran in and grabbed a clean wet cloth for Greg to clean off his shoes. He quickly did, handed me the cloth and left. When I returned to the house, Cal stood there in the middle of the living room grinning like the cat that ate the canary. I shook my head. He snickered and vanished.

Though I felt kind of sorry for Greg, I couldn't help but chuckle. Apparently Cal, the little stinker, had known Greg was coming. I couldn't be mad at him, though. He did it for me.

It was Sunday night and Mom had gone home after having a pot roast dinner with me. She hadn't gone to evening worship at the church. It was only eight when she left, and I wasn't in any mood to go to bed so early. I walked down to Nancy's and Paul's apartment. Their lights were out though and I remembered then that they were out with some pagan friends. I had just forgotten. I glanced over at the park, as it was always lit fairly well along the sidewalk, and thought of going and sitting on the bench that faced Dad's church, as services were in process there. "But why do I want to do that?" I asked myself. It hit me then that I was just lonely. Though Mom was back and I had a few friends, I was still very lonely. "Oh heck with it!" I went back to my apartment and decided to take a nice long hot bath instead of a shower. Afterwards, perhaps I would find a good movie somewhere.

I ran my water as hot as I could stand it and sank down up to my neck and just let myself soak. I closed my eyes and tried not to think of anything. The next thing I knew, I woke up with my water freezing cold. I got out as quickly as I could, shivering. I wrapped myself in my white, terrycloth robe and let the water out. I went on to my bedroom and there slipped into my shorty pajamas and climbed into bed. Still sleepy, I soon drifted off.

Sometime in the middle of the night, I dreamed I was in bed with this handsome blond-headed man. He had his arm around me from behind. He kissed my neck and my cheek and cuddled up to me. I know I reacted to his touch, letting out little sighs of pleasure. Then I was aware of his hand flat on my tummy, pressing gently.

My eyes popped open. The hand was still there. I slowly slid my hand down and felt *his* – Wasn't imaging it! I gasped and sat up, turning to face *him* in the darkened room. I could barely make out the luminous outline of his perfect frame.

He spoke softly, "Hello, Brenda."

"Paleo?"

"None other." He then made himself more visible for me, shining in a soft, radiant bluish white. "I sensed your loneliness again. You are lonely, aren't you?"

He was right. I was damn lonely. As beautiful as he was, I was still a little leery. Had to admit, though, that the mere touch of his hand was nothing short of wonderful. "A little," I admitted.

"Still unsure of me, aren't you? But that's okay. It takes time."

"I'm not sure—."

"Of having a sexual relationship with a demon," he finished for me.

He was partly right, but that wasn't all of it. "I'm actually not sure I want a relationship with any male right now."

"Would you prefer a succubus?" He asked matter-of-factly.

My jaw dropped. "Oh! No! I didn't mean that at all."

An amused chuckle came from deep in his chest. "Good! Because I would hope you would choose me, if you decide you want a physical relationship."

I feasted my eyes over his perfectly formed body – though luminous blue was a bit distracting – and peered into his sparkling even bluer eyes. "Your head's perfectly shaped," I suddenly blurted, not sure why I did.

He laughed. "Is that all that you take notice of?"

"Oh! No! I… I actually have never seen anyone so beautiful," I quietly replied, feasting my eyes over him – no armor this time – the smoothness of his off-white skin, and the perfectly formed muscles, resembling a living statue of marble. I was really wondering what sex would be like with him. And here he was, apparently more than willing to teach me.

"I'm not going to push myself on you, Brenda. I want you to want me too."

I am not sure why, but I knew he spoke the truth. It was just something I felt. "I trust you."

"Good." He stood, towering over me. He lowered his face down to where our lips were very close. "Would it be all right if I kissed you?"

I was beginning to feel that tingling sensation all over my body. I remembered the energy thing, but this time it didn't seem as strong as before. "I… I guess so."

"Is that a yes?"

I bobbed my head in the affirmative. "Yes!" I waited in anticipation, as his eyes studied mine, and he slowly pressed his oh-so-soft lips gently to mine. They were warm, and his kiss was sweet and unhurried – and buzzing! Kind of tickled. I couldn't help but respond. We kissed for a good minute before he pulled his face back.

"Okay?" he inquired.

"Very." The energy, the tingling, was stronger. In fact, my body was buzzing pretty much all over, especially in my private areas.

He knew this. "The buzzing is perfectly normal. It is because we are so close. Any demon standing so close will make you buzz, especially one of the opposite sex."

"Okay… That's nice to know." I was excited, amused and apprehensive all at the same time.

"Tell you what. I'll let you think about it some more."

"…Okay." I appreciated his consideration, but I was uncertain if I wanted him to go or not. Part of me was still hesitant to go any further with him, but the other part was really kind of needing him. And not just sex. It is hard to explain. But I suddenly needed to have sex with him! I knew no human male could satisfy this need I was suddenly feeling. "What's happening to me?" I asked.

He understood perfectly. "Your body's energy is increasing with your meditations, making it easier for you to tolerate the presence of demons."

"Yes. Go on please."

"Demons can satisfy humans in ways that other humans can't. I believe you sense that. I can reach parts of you a human male can't… It is the same with a succubus and a human male. I can satisfy you without you ever physically climaxing."

"Oh?"

"Yes! When we climax it is spiritual. It is a blending of our souls. It is the most beautiful feeling, sensation you could ever possibly experience."

Somehow I knew he wasn't just saying it. "Okay…"

"But I don't want to pressure you. I want to be one with you… and only you, for as long as you live… And then some. However, if you wish to be able to have a physical relationship with a human too, I can abide by that. Not what I prefer, but I can accept what is natural for you."

"I'm not sure, Paleo. I think I kind of understand. Can we just leave that part open for now? I mean…"

"I understand. Leave the option open for you to have a human partner as well. I can do that."

"I'm thinking that I want children."

"I also understand that. And it is okay."

"Right now, there's no one else though."

"I know."

"You said until I die. What happens after I die? Will I see you then?"

"Yes! But you will no longer be human, and our relationship will be a little different, but there's no point into going into that now. If you are reincarnated, we can be together again. In fact, we can be together for many lifetimes, if we want."

"Wow! I had no idea."

"Tell you what. I will leave you for now and let you think about everything."

"Okay. I wasn't sure I wanted him to go, but I also wasn't sure I was quite ready."

He kissed the tip of my nose then and vanished, but I heard him clearly in my head. "I won't be far, sweetheart."

"All right!"

*

We were really busy at the library for the next week, giving me little time to think about Paleo, but think about him I did anyway, when I had a free moment. More shipments of books had come in. Also, we were clearing out a lot of old books that were being replaced by new copies and were having a book sale, and Miranda put me in charge. We were selling books for as low as twenty-five cents each.

We started off with two tables loaded down, but by afternoon it all fit on one table. I was so busy I barely had time to eat lunch.

When five o'clock rolled around and it was time to get off, I was exhausted. Mom had texted earlier that she was picking up some Kentucky Fried Chicken and she would meet me at my apartment.

I wasn't home fifteen minutes and she knocked on the door. I let her in and she rushed into my little kitchen with the chicken and sides of mashed potatoes, biscuits and coleslaw and sat them on the table. I already had our iced tea, plates and silverware ready. I thanked her and told her that it would be my turn next to buy dinner.

With a grin, she agreed and pulled out a chair and settled down in it. I handed her a napkin and we filled our plates. She was in a very good mood, and I questioned her about it. I thought maybe she had met some nice doctor that was single, but that was not the case. She was just really happy with her new job, and felt blessed that we were together again.

She did say that she had seen Dad earlier, had gone by to pick up some clothes that she had left there, hoping he still had them. He did, and she was happy about that. She let me know she had seen Greg too. He was polite and all, but it was pretty obvious that he was depressed. She admitted that she almost felt sorry for him. "I really do not believe he is as bad as your father, Brenda," she said, as she blotted her face with a napkin and set it aside.

"I know, Mom. But he is still of the mindset that women should 'obey' their husbands, etc. And I don't… can't live with that anymore."

"I know, sugar. He does still love you. I honestly question if your father ever really loved me, though."

"Oh I think he loved you as much as he could love anyone."

She kind of chuckled and looked down, playing with her napkin. "But not the way I needed him to love me." She turned her eyes back up to me. "Greg does love you that way, you know?"

"Mom, are you trying to tell me something here?"

She scrunched up her lips momentarily before replying. "Yes. I suppose I am."

"You don't seriously want me to go back to him, do you?"

"That's just it… I'm not sure. But seeing how much he loves you… and you do love him, don't you?"

"Not like I used to. But yes, I still have feelings for him. Why?"

"I don't know. It's just that you did marry him. And you really haven't been married that long. He loves you so much. I just can't help but wonder if maybe it could work?" She eyed me kind of sheepishly. "I know it sounds really kind of ludicrous coming from someone who didn't want you to get married right away, but, fact is, you did marry him."

"I know, Mom. And believe me I have thought about it a lot. When I see him look at me with such hurt, it does bother me… immensely." I shook my head. "But I know now that being married to a preacher is not what I want! Not anymore. I have changed too much."

She pushed her napkin aside, brow furrowed. "What do you mean by that?"

"I'll come out and say it. I don't believe in the church anymore. I don't believe what is taught. Mom, I'm not a Christian anymore!"

"What?" Even for her, this was shocking. "But you were raised a Christian? I admit that we were strict. Too strict. But surely you haven't lost your faith in God?"

I pushed away from the table. "Mom, I don't want to discuss this now." Shaking, I stood and went to the window over the sink and looked out. It was clouding up outside. Looked like rain.

"You *do* believe in God, don't you?"

"Let it go, Mom."

"Come back and finish your dinner, hon."

"I can't…won't… discuss it anymore."

"Okay. I guess you feel that I have betrayed you. I left you because you wanted to marry Greg, and now I'm suggesting you go back to him. I am sorry! I've had a little time to see things from a different perspective. So, I was just telling you my viewpoint now. Please come back and finish your dinner. I promise to not talk about it. Please?"

I let out a long sigh and turned around. "All right. Tell me about your work."

With a smile of relief, she said, "I'd love to."

The air was still a little tense for a while, but as we talked about our jobs the hurtful feelings fled away.

After Mom left, I wondered if she was having second thoughts about having left Dad. She did tell me that the divorce had not been finalized yet. There was still another month before she had to appear in court. She also admitted that though it wasn't the main reason she had come back, she also had to come back to be there for the divorce. I was glad she told me. Had I found out without her letting me know, and had I not seen how much she seemed to have missed me, I might have thought that it was the primary reason she had returned.

Chapter Thirteen

It was Friday night and Nancy and Paul came in the library right before closing, wanting me to come by their apartment when I got off at five. I let them know that Mom had asked me to come over to her place later, have dinner and watch a movie on television, and I had said I would.

My friends shared a glance, smiling and turned back to me. Nancy spoke, "We just want to show you something. Can you drop by for a few minutes first… before going to your mothers?"

"I suppose I can," I replied, seeing that it seemed kind of important to them. "I'll call Mom and tell her I will be a few minutes late. I'm sure she will understand."

"Awesome!" Paul said, giving me a wink. "We'll see you in a little while."

They turned and left. I checked out a boy in his early teens, and then a middle-aged black lady behind him. That seemed to be the only ones ready to check out books. I glanced over at Miranda. She gave me a cheerful nod and said I could go. I thanked her, grabbed my purse and left. I did go home first, combed my hair, brushed my teeth and freshened up my makeup before walking down to Paul's and Nancy's.

Nancy was all smiles when she opened the door. "Thanks for coming on such short notice."

"Not a problem." My eyes went to Paul who was sitting back on their sofa, with his right arm stretched out across the back.

"We wanted you to be the first to know," Nancy said as she sat down beside Paul and snuggled up to his side.

My eyes darted back and forth from Nancy to Paul and then back to Nancy. "Know what?" Paul waved for me to take a seat in the easy chair. So I did.

Nancy stuck her hand out for me to see. A beautiful ring with a larger diamond than what I might have anticipated sparkled out at me. I am sure my eyes widened at the surprise.

"You're engaged?"

Paul sat forward then and smiled lovingly to Nancy before speaking. "Yep! Surprised her with it when she got up this morning."

"Had the day off," Nancy said. "Paul brought my breakfast to me while I was still in bed. And sitting on my napkin was a beautiful black box and inside was this ring. I am amazed you didn't hear me scream in surprise."

"Yep. Damn near burst my eardrums," Paul agreed with an ear-to-ear grin.

Her happiness was catching. I was thrilled for her, for the both of them. "That is so awesome!"

He reached over and squeezed her right hand. "We agree that we probably won't ever find anyone else to suit us the way we do one another. I'd been giving it some serious thought for several weeks. I made some extra money on some especially extravagant websites and thought… what the hey! Why not? I went down to Zales and picked out the ring."

My eyes misted. "I am *so* happy for the both of you!" I knew by the gleam in her eyes though that she couldn't be happier. And I felt that they were definitely perfect for one another.

"We want you to stand up for us when we get married," Nancy said.

"We talked it over," Paul said. "We don't want a big wedding… Have this thing about churches." He grinned amusedly. "And we've been living together for a while now. Just want to make it legal. Have a quick ceremony at the courthouse. We want you to witness for us. Then later, we want do a ritual devoting our marriage to Father Satan, and we want you to come."

"I would be honored. I wouldn't miss it for anything."

That made both of them happy.

Nancy jumped up and came over to me, giving me a hug. "I don't have many friends, and neither does Paul. At least not ones who really know about us and live close. Having you living close to us is great. Your friendship is very important." She sat back down.

"As yours is to me… When do you plan on tying the knot?"

They shared a look and then back to me, and Paul answered, "December the twenty-third."

I thought about it a moment and then realized the significance of the date. "Oh! Father Satan's day of the year! That is so cool!"

Looking lovingly to Paul but speaking to me, Nancy said, "Paul asked me when I wanted to get married. Offered for us to get married right away. But it is only a few months away. And Father has been so good to us. I couldn't think of a better time."

"Nor could I, when she told me," Paul said. "In fact, I'm kind of miffed at myself for not thinking of it too."

"That is so cool! And I couldn't be happier for the both of you." I glanced at my watch. Mom would have dinner about ready.

Seeing my action, Paul said, "We know you need to get going, but thank you so much for stopping by."

"Hey… My pleasure." I stood, and so did they, going to the door with me.

Nancy hugged me again, and then it was Paul's turn. He gave me a strong hug and a kiss on the cheek.

"I'll see you later," I said and walked out. I seriously could not have been happier for them. I only wished that my marriage had been different, that we could have been suited for one another the way Nancy and Paul were. But I knew that that was not the case. In fact, I wasn't sure I could or would ever be happy with a man again. Not a human one, anyway.

Mom and I had a good dinner and enjoyed watching *The Day the Earth Stood Still,* the original one in black and white with Michael Rennie. I had seen it a number of times, and also the newer one with Keanu Reeves, but I liked them both.

Later, by the time I arrived home, I was tired and ready for bed and very glad that I did not have to get up early. I was working the afternoon shift at the library and could sleep in.

By the time I had my shower and slipped into bed it was five minutes of midnight. I thought I would go right to sleep, but I didn't. I just laid there thinking about how excited Nancy and Paul were, which brought back memories of when Greg and I first married. Though I had been truly happy for a while – thought I was anyway – I do not believe I was ever as happy as my friends were.

The longer I lay there, the lonelier I felt. I tossed this way and that and couldn't seem to get comfortable. The next thing I knew, it was one in the morning. "Shit!" I hissed before thinking about it. It seemed that I had gotten into the habit of saying that word a lot lately. Before, in all the years of growing up, I never swore or said anything worse than darn. Now, it seemed the word shit just slipped out involuntarily when something upset or bugged me.

I lay there a while longer, glancing at the continuously changing of seconds on my alarm clock. Then I detected a warmth over the center of my tummy. It was hardly detectable at first, but then it grew warmer and warmer until there was no denying it. I moved my hand down to feel what I now expected – another hand! "You're back," I said in a near whisper.

"I felt your loneliness and therefore was compelled to comfort you."

I thought about it a second. "That's really sweet of you."

"Thank you," he replied. "But it could also be construed that I very much would like to fulfill your need to be loved."

I grinned to myself. "Sex, you mean." By the time the words left my mouth, I also felt something else behind me… It wasn't a totally unfamiliar feeling. One I had felt from my estranged husband many a time. I am not sure exactly why I did, but I rolled over to face him. His beautiful eyes shone into mine and I could vaguely make out that he was smiling. I wondered that I could only barely see him, but I most definitely could feel him.

He knew my thoughts and said, "That's just the way it is. We can touch humans easier than we can make ourselves visible, even though we can fully materialize, but it takes a lot of energy. I cannot tell you exactly why that is."

I reached up with my left hand and touched the side of his face. It was warm – actually kind of hot – soft and so very, very smooth. "From what I can see, you are amazingly beautiful."

"Thank you. I will consider that a compliment. However, in this form, our kind finds one another kind of boring, as we all look so much alike."

"You do?"

"Yes. In this state, we have no hair, but we are very similar to humans otherwise. We find hair very attractive on humans, as we do on our own. In our natural state, we look very human. It is the shape of our eyes that holds the most difference."

"Interesting," I noted. Then before I could even have another thought, he kissed me, fully, passionately and demandingly. I know I gasped when he pulled his lips away from mine. I swallowed hard.

"You okay?"

"…Ah. I think so." I quivered.

"I can go, if you want me to?"

I'm not sure why, but I suddenly sat up and swung my legs over the side of the bed. He quickly moved over and sat up beside me, laying a hand on my shoulder. "I will ask again. Do you want me to leave?"

I turned and stared into those captivating eyes that I so easily could have gotten lost in. Such depths! I could almost see the universe in them. "I'm not really sure."

"Tell you what. Just lie down again. I will lie down behind you, like we were before."

I slowly did as he said, and he snuggled up to me from behind and placed his arm around me, holding my tummy again. I have to admit, he felt absolutely wonderful: The feathery warmth, the energy from his body so softly wrapped around mine – was like a warm fire on a cold winter's night. I've never known anything so absolutely amazing. I could have laid there forever with his warmness wrapped around me like that. I am pretty sure that I actually cooed.

We lay there for several minutes while I simply relished the awesome touch of his energy, his body, enshrouding mine. Then, before I actually realized what was happening, there was this wonderful sensation deep inside me. My eyes widened. I was being touched inside in a way I was sure no human male could ever do. The delicate but titillating sensation, the beautiful indescribable feeling, grew and grew in intensity until I could stand it no longer, and he knew this and responded immediately, making love to me in the wildest yet gentlest way that one could never imagine. One has to experience it to truly understand.

I am not sure how long we made love, but I was uplifted to a wondrous place of absolute, sensuous perfection, and when he at last climaxed, I climaxed with him, but it was completely different from anything I had shared with my husband. It went through my entire body, flooding through my very soul! A thrill such as is indescribable, and then there was another surge of this blissfulness, and again, one more time. I know I cried out in rapture. I could not help it.

After we finished, I lay there completely shaken from such profound ecstasy, and I was in somewhat of a state of shock for several minutes, totally and utterly speechless.

I had never experienced anything so completely beautiful in my entire life. Tears of utter joy filled my eyes. I reached up and wiped one off my cheek.

"Was that to your satisfaction, my sweet?" he asked.

"Oh my God!" I managed and rolled over to face him. I searched his wondrous eyes. I saw only beauty there and a desire to please me. Then I whispered, "I have never... ever... in my entire life had a clue that anything could ever be so... so splendorous!"

"I am happy you find me sufficient."

"Sufficient? Jeeze! That was the most awesome experience anyone could ever have... ever!"

He smiled hugely. "I am glad I was able to satisfy you."

"If you call that beyond amazing experience satisfaction, then yes! You definitely satisfied me!"

"That is all I want, my darling. My only desire is to please you."

"Not a problem." I was having a bit of trouble understanding his humbleness. "You are freakin' awesome! And that doesn't even begin to describe how wonderful you are!"

He kissed the tip of my nose. "Now you should get some rest. I will lie here with you, if that is okay?"

"Oh it is most definitely ok." I rolled over and he gently laid his arm around me again, once more with his hand resting on my belly. I went right to sleep.

Paleo was gone when I awoke, but that was okay. I knew he couldn't stay with me twenty-four-seven.

I practically waltzed into work, still feeling uplifted by the most beautiful night of my life. Miranda noticed my happy mood right away; turning from the books she was checking out and smiling broadly. "You're mighty cheery, girl."

"That is an understatement. I don't know when I have ever been happier!" I replied, and then realized she would assume what she did.

"Ah! You meet some special guy?"

I was caught off guard and couldn't think of anything else to say, so I said, "Something like that."

"Good for you!" She turned back to checking out the young blonde facing her.

I didn't know what I was going to tell her later, though. Whatever I told her would have to be a lie. There was no way I could tell her that I had an incubus! And that being with him was the most amazing thing that had ever happened to me. I was totally convinced there was no way anything could ever be more beautiful. I felt like the prettiest, luckiest girl in the world. I knew that I would never want anyone else after being with Paleo.

A couple of days and nights went by, and I didn't hear from Paleo. I admit I was kind of disappointed, but he had told me he was a soldier, therefore I understood that I could not expect him to be with me twenty-four-seven.

Mom kept me occupied, and we had dinner together almost every evening when I worked days. One night I would eat at her apartment, the next, she would eat at mine. That is, except for Sunday nights. In spite of her disappointment in her marriage, she was still a Christian. That she had not given up entirely.

On Tuesday night, though, Nancy and Paul asked me over for pizza. I knew Mom would be expecting to eat with me, but I didn't want to tell my friends no. So when Mom called, I told her my neighbors had invited me over for Pizza. She said that was okay, but could she see me later? I told her that would be fine, that I would text or call her when I got home.

I thoroughly enjoyed my visit with Nancy and Paul. Paul was all enthused about a new Satanic website he was building and couldn't wait to show it to me. I have to admit it was impressive. It was about as thorough as the best websites out there, but instead of a black and red theme, his was black and a vibrant blue, since blue is also one of Father Satan's colors.

He let me know that he had every intention of making it the best possible website he could. He admired all the work others had had put into their websites, but wanted to do his part in spreading the truth to the world about our Father Satan.

"I have to hand it to you," I told him. "I am impressed!"

Nancy had been standing by him at the computer. She hugged his arm. "Yes! My guy is pretty awesome!"

She was so obvious. She loved her man. "Yes he is."

My phone rang. It was Mom. Probably worrying that I had forgotten she wanted to come over. I answered her and told her I would be home in about five minutes. That made her happy, and she cheerfully stated that she was on her way.

Paul handed me a flier he had made up promoting his website. I thanked him, folded it up and stuck it in the back pocket of my jeans. I then helped them clean up the table, bid them goodnight and left.

Mom pulled in just as I unlocked my door. When I pushed the door open, I caught a glimpse of Cal standing in the middle of the living room. This time, he wasn't grinning like the Cheshire cat in Alice in Wonderland. He seemed concerned about something. I frowned inquisitively, but Mom walked up and he disappeared.

"Enjoy your pizza?" she asked; all smiles as she breezed in behind me. She tossed her brown leather handbag on the sofa.

"Yes! Enjoyed it very much." I headed for the refrigerator. "Want a Coke?"

"Sure. Haven't had one today. Sounds good."

I grabbed one for each of us and pulled the tab off mine and set it aside. I would toss it in the trash later. She did the same with hers.

"You eat?" I enquired.

"I grabbed a burger at Burger King."

"I'm sorry about tonight, Mom, but I don't get asked over for dinner often with my friends."

She smiled amiably. "Pshaw! Think nothing of it. I know you need your friends. Everyone does. Unfortunately, the only friends I have around here are the ones from the church." She sipped on her Coke, and then said, "Actually, I take that back. I am making friends at work... Not close though. Not yet."

"Surely you will in time."

I had forgotten about the flier Paul had handed me, and it must have fallen out of my pocket when I sat down. It was blood red and quite noticeable. I think I realized it was on the floor at the same time Mom did. "What's that?" she asked, leaning forward to snatch it up. I tried to grab it first, but was unsuccessful.

"I'm sure it's nothing," I lied. "Found it on the walk and stuffed it in my pocket. Haven't had a chance to really look at it."

She unfolded it and stared briefly before her eyes got huge. She looked up at me. "Brenda! This is promoting a Satanic website! Did you know that?"

"…I noticed something about that. Like I said, haven't had a chance to read it."

The furrows in her brow grew deeper as she read the paper. Then her face flushed almost as red as the flier. "This is absolute trash!" She wadded the paper in her hand and immediately got up and threw it away in my garbage can under the sink. She came back in and plopped down, eyeing me strangely.

"What?"

"Please tell me you're not hanging out with a bunch of Satanists?"

"Where is this coming from? I told you I didn't read it. I just found it and hadn't really looked at it yet."

"It is obvious that it is Satanic, though. Why did you even keep it?"

"It was on the sidewalk. I don't like to see people leave trash on the sidewalk, Mom."

I could tell by her expression that she had doubts that I was telling the truth. She knew me too well. "Your father told me about your venture with Wiccans."

"History, Mom! Been there… done that. Over!"

"I certainly hope so."

"Did he tell you that he tried to exorcise a demon out of me?"

An embarrassed frown came to her face. "Yes. I let him know that that was a terrible thing to do to you."

"Really? That's all you said?"

"He agreed that it was extreme, but he felt he had no choice. In fact, he's not entirely sure it worked. He now believes that you were acting when the demon supposedly came out of you… Is that true? You're not 'acting' now, are you?"

I admit I was now a little more than pissed at the way my mother was reacting, especially after all the years of crap she went through with my father, and leaving us the way she did. "Aren't you being just a little hypocritical?" I tartly asked.

I think the anger in my voice startled her. Surprise was written all over her face. "How's that?"

"Your hatred of Dad's holier than thou ways. You couldn't stand his extreme devotion to the church. You left us high and dry. Now you sit there and have a fit because of a flier about a Satanic website?"

"I see no connection, Brenda. What's your point?"

"I think there's a huge point – Your marriage was one big joke! Dad professes to be a man of God, but treated you like crap! You call that Godly?"

She tried to speak, but I interrupted her.

"Father thinks he's a prophet of God or something. And Greg is getting there. They preach love and forgiveness. But do you see love in Dad? Do you? You see any real forgiveness? Has he realized why you left him?"

"Not actually."

"Even Greg. I know he's tried in his own way, but he still doesn't quite get it."

"Want to clarify that?"

"I shouldn't have to. You know why you left. What gives them the right to judge us? Doesn't the Bible say, 'Judge not that you be judged?' Yet those two pricks go around thumping their Bibles and pointing fingers and making accusations. But do they know what is really going on in a person's head? In a person's heart? No! They are breaking one of their God's rules! And right now, I believe you are being just a bit judgmental too!"

"Brenda!" She sat her Coke down on the coffee table. "I know how your father is. And there is no way I want to go back to that, but I haven't lost my faith... Looks to me like you have. Have you? I'm sorry. Maybe I am being a little judgmental. I can't help it, knowing that you were raised a Christian! And what do you mean by 'their God's rules'?"

"What I said. He's their God. Not mine."

"Then pray tell, just who is *your* God?"

"I simply mean I do not believe the way the church teaches. I believe in a God who loves us. Not one who condemns us for every little thing. Sex, for one! When he made us with the desire for sex and then condemns anyone for having those feelings! Pluck your eye out if you look at a woman the wrong way! What kind of scripture is that? We are human!"

"That's why Jesus laid down his life for us," she responded, flustered now. "We can't be perfect."

"You really believe that a truly loving God would sacrifice his own son in cold blood?"

"Brenda!"

"Mom! It is a lie! The dying and reviving God idea was stolen from numerous mythologies! The scholars will tell you that Jesus wasn't born on December twenty-fifth! The date was set close to the winter solstice. They believe he was born in September. That is, if he even really existed? There are quite a few who believe that he is an entirely fictional character. Myself, I believe he was a guru, a very wise one, but human, of course. After all, they murdered him for going against their Jewish taught lies."

"Brenda! Oh my God! I don't believe I am hearing this!" She stood and grabbed up her purse.

"So now you are going to walk out on me because I speak the truth?"

"You don't know that."

"Yes I do! Don't take my word for it. Do the research. I have. The whole Jewish, Christian, Muslim thing is nothing more than a glorified lie! A lie perpetuated to control the masses!"

I have never seen my mother so upset with me, but I had to say what was in my heart. I had to say the truth! "I won't listen to any more of this! I can't believe this is coming from my own daughter! Now I see I was wrong in leaving you! I didn't really believe your father when he told me you were a lost soul. But now I see he might have been right, for once!" She ran out and slammed the door.

I swung the door open and screamed, "You hypocrite!" Then I slammed my door so hard the windows rattled, and then I locked it. When I turned back around, Cal was sitting on the sofa, sadly shaking his head. "Sorry, Brenda." He gave the cushion next to him a pat.

I sat down beside him, and he put his short little arm around me the best he could.

"You knew this was going to happen, didn't you?"

He wriggled his head yes.

I couldn't help it. I cried, and I cried hard for some time. But my little friend stayed right with me until I finally calmed down.

"You all better now?" he asked after a while.

"I think so," I replied.

"Good. I go now. But I come if you need me."

"Thank you, Cal."

He vanished, and I went off to take my shower before going to bed. I felt numb all over and hoped to fall into the blessed blackness of sleep. However, a few minutes after I slipped under my bed covers I felt this warmth wrap around me. My first thought was that it was Paleo, but after a minute or two I realized the hug was different. It was more of a fatherly hug. I felt it all through my being, and I can't explain it but I knew that it was Father Satan hugging me this time. I never felt so loved and cherished in my entire life. It too was like lying in front of a warm fire on a cold winter night. It is a feeling that no one could ever forget. It was so purely peaceful. He lay there with me until I fell asleep.

When I awoke the next morning there was a text on my phone from Mom saying she was sorry about our tiff the night before, that Dad had had her all worked up, and when she saw the flier she had feared that maybe there were some grounds for his accusations. She hoped I would forgive her and have dinner with her at Denny's when I got off. Though somewhat reluctant and still feeling more than a little hurt, I replied back that all was forgiven and accepted her invitation to dinner.

Even though I felt a little more at ease considering she had apologized, there was still that uncertainty as to what she would do if she really knew. How could I ever make her understand just how wonderful Father Satan truly is? For no one can know unless they do dedicate to him. No one had to tell me that we were a long, long way from that ever happening. Though rebellious to being controlled and subservient to the male gender, she still had far too much of the 'Christian' ideals (lies to control) for that to happen.

Of course, I hoped for her sake that one day she would come to know the truth, but it was something she would have to find on her own. The truth is all around, once one takes off the blindfolds and begins to listen to reason.

Unfortunately, so many have been brainwashed so long and so steadily that they can't see the truth when it hits them in the face.

Still, I hoped. She's my mother.

Chapter Fourteen

Though Paleo came to see me as often as he could, there were still times when two or three nights went by that he didn't. When that was the case, I would simply lie in bed thinking of him and hoping he could come soon. His love-making was so far beyond wonderful that each night I would ready for bed in excited anticipation that this night might be a night that he would again take me beyond the stars and wondrous realms of imagination. I could hardly wait.

I loved Paleo so much I could no longer keep it to myself. I finally gave in to the need to tell someone and I told Nancy and Paul.

They were thrilled for me. Paul said he had a male friend who had a succubus, and claimed she was beyond his wildest dreams. Both Nancy and Paul confessed that should they ever lose one another that they would probably consider having a demon lover. Still, like me, they would probably leave things open just in case they did meet someone human of the opposite sex; someone that they would want to be with. That is, unless they were up in years. In that case, they would be very happy without a human lover and be very happy with an incubus or succubus.

Paleo never told me anything of his duties as a soldier, only that he had been on duty or had to leave for duty. He always seemed very happy to be with me, though. That, in itself, made me deliriously happy. I would have never thought that I could love a supernatural creature, especially an incubus! There are so many horrible stories and lies about them out there. When in actuality, they are some of the most wonderful beings a human could ever have the privilege and honor of knowing. I thank Father Satan daily for Paleo.

Mom and I were back to as 'normal' a relationship as possible, with her being an ingrained Christian. In spite of her differences with Dad, she was now attending services regularly. This, of course, according to her (and I'm sure it was true), made Dad very happy. I did warn her when we were having dinner at my apartment one Wednesday evening before service that Dad might take it as a sign she wanted to return to their marriage.

To my surprise, she kind of blew it off. "Oh well… If he wants to think that, let him," she replied, smiling a though it weren't a big deal. "I have no intentions of going back to him. I've told him so too."

"I know you have. But he is a man, and may think that you are letting him know that you aren't going to be easily obtainable this time. He may think you are putting up a front because you think you can set up some rules of your own. That you are playing hard to get."

Her brow narrowed slightly and she waved her hand dismissively. "Oh I don't believe he thinks that."

"I wouldn't be so sure, Mom. Dad's too cocky. I think he thinks you want to come back to him. He still thinks he's one of God's gifts to mankind. And that includes his wife."

She let out a soft laugh. "Well, I do agree with that last statement." She put out a hand then. "Hey! Why don't you come to church with me this evening?"

This I had not anticipated. "What?"

"You heard me. Come to church with me?"

"I don't think so." I pushed my chair back and took my plate and set it in the sink, and then turned to face her. She had stood too and put her plate in the sink as well.

"Why not?" She eyed me curiously.

"I told you before. I don't believe that way anymore."

"You do believe in God, don't you?"

"I do believe in a God," I replied. "Just not in the controlling, hellfire and brimstone-thrower that you do."

Anger surfaced in her eyes. She went to speak, but then must have remembered our last fight. She sighed and glanced off momentarily before addressing me. "All right. I don't want us to fight again. I just thought it would be nice if you came to church with me."

"Even if I wanted to go to church – which I don't – I would not step inside a church that dragged me across the yard and spent hours trying to exorcise a demon out of me!"

There was a flicker of pain in her eyes. "Oh! I forgot about that... Okay. I guess I can understand you not wanting to go there. I'm so sorry."

"It's okay, Mom. If you want to attend, fine. I don't have a problem with it. Just don't expect me to."

"Maybe I shouldn't go either?" she said with a far-off look. "But I wouldn't feel at home anywhere else." Her expression was that she was hoping to see approval from me for her to go.

"I said it was okay. Go on, Mom. I know you miss your old friends. But keep in mind they're not mine. Not anymore."

"I have to say that is very generous of you, considering the circumstances. I am sure they thought they were doing the right thing though."

"I'm sure they did... in their ignorance."

She flinched at my words but didn't address it. Instead, she said, "I'll help you with these dishes and then go."

"It's okay, Mom. I glanced at my watch. You will be late if you help me. Besides, there aren't that many dishes for just the two of us."

"You're sure?"

"Absolutely. Go ahead."

"Okay, hon. I'll call you tomorrow."

"Okay. Bye."

"Bye, hon. Have a good evening." She kissed my cheek.

"You too."

She left. I was relieved that our argument was settled before it got out of hand; that Mom had had the reasoning to stop when she did. Also, I had Paleo on my mind. I hoped, oh how I hoped, he could come see me. I really needed for him to hold me.

It was too early to go to bed though, and church would be getting under way soon. It was still warm enough in the evenings that I didn't need a jacket yet, so I decided to take a walk in the park. As I approached the bench that faced opposite the church, I saw a familiar figure sitting on the far end of the bench – Erick! Seeing me, he smiled and said hello. I said hello back and took a seat by him.

"How are you this fine evening?" he asked.

"Good, I guess. Mom and I almost had a fight, but then she managed to shut her mouth before it got out of hand."

"Yes. I thought that was your mother leaving your apartment a few minutes ago. You two look a lot alike."

"So I've been told. Thanks. I consider that a compliment."

"I meant it as one. Your mother is a very attractive woman."

"I'm sure my mother would be thrilled if she heard you say that."

Musical sounds of a hymn wafted its way across the street. I recognized it right away as a favorite one from my childhood: *Revive Us Again.* I guess I will always love the hymn, even if that's not the way I believe anymore. I did get teary-eyed. And I hated the fact that what the churches taught simply wasn't so. That so many were raised to believe the untruths. It wasn't just Christianity either. It all originated when the Jews wanted the world to believe they were God's 'chosen' people, and then there were the Muslims. It was all a profoundly crazy joke on mankind. Hearing the hymn brought very painful, mixed feelings to the surface. I began sobbing.

Instantly, Erick laid a comforting arm around me.

"It hurts," I said. "It all hurts so much."

"I know," he replied, seeming to understand fully what I was experiencing. "But someday the truth will come out."

I looked up at him with a start. "You know?"

I could swear his eyes glowed unnaturally. "I know, Brenda."

I had accused him once of being supernatural, so I wasn't about to do it again. Still, at that moment, I had the distinct feeling that I had been right to begin with. Maybe he just couldn't or didn't want to admit it to me. At least, not yet.

After the hymn ended, I could hear my father offering up a prayer, as he had a voice that carried well. Something that was good for a man of his profession. After the prayer, he began his sermon, and as I sat there hearing the condemnations and accusations and my father telling everyone they were going to burn in some fiery hell if they didn't confess their sins right then and there and beg God for forgiveness, my sadness turned back to anger.

Erick apparently saw this. "All better now?" he asked with a slight grin tilting the corners of his mouth.

"Yeah… Yeah… Thanks."

He withdrew his arm. "Not a problem." He sucked in air then and let it out in a long sigh.

I stood. I'd had enough of the sermon going on across the street. "I guess I'll head back home now."

Erick stood too. "I'll walk you home."

"Thanks. But you don't have to."

"I know, Brenda. I want to. That is, if it's okay with you?"

"Sure! I just didn't want you to feel like you had to."

"I don't. But it is dark. And I would feel better myself knowing you arrived home safely."

"Since you put it that way… By all means, please walk me home."

Grinning in his charming way, he held out a hand for me to lead the way, and we headed for my apartment.

To my disappointment, once more Paleo failed to come. I knew that he would when he could though. So I swallowed my disappointment and managed to fall asleep.

*

I sniffed. Something tickled the tip of my nose. I sniffed again and rubbed the bottom of my nose with my forefinger. I started to drift back to sleep, but then ever so slightly something tickled my nose again. My eyes popped open and I saw the back of Cal's dark blue hoodie as he dashed out my bedroom door. A white feather drifting to the floor also caught my eye. I sat up. "Cal! You little stinker!" I scrambled to my feet and went after him. Wasn't anywhere to be seen. "You little twit!"

Distinct cackling.

"Darn you, Cal!"

I heard muffled laughter again, but something told me he wasn't going to let himself get caught. I rolled my eyes and headed for my coffee pot. It was time to get up anyway. "Little turd," I mumbled to myself. At least, Cal made my life more interesting. I never knew when he was going to pull one of his little pranks. It was just all in fun for him. He would never do anything to harm me. He would defend me without any qualms. He'd already proven that when he saved me that night in the park.

I drank my coffee, dressed for work and looked outside the living room window. Rain was pouring down. Today, I would take my car to work. It probably needed to be run anyway, as I walked most of the places I went, which was work primarily, and then the park. "Gee," I said to myself. "My life is so eventful these days. But it beats the hell out of being Dad's and Greg's slave." I breathed, "And then there's Cal… and Paleo. Now they do make a difference."

I opened my door to walk out, and just I went to close it, I heard Cal say, "Glad to be of help!" A slight snigger followed. I laughed to myself and locked the door. I knew Cal could get out. He was able to slip through dimensions somehow. I never questioned him about it, but I knew that was true. A lot of the time he would be only partly in my dimension, as I would see just kind of an outline of him. Other times, he would fully appear. And then he would completely disappear on me, especially when he was playing one of his mischievous tricks. I thought it really cool.

Mom dropped by the library just before it was time for me to get off and let me know she wouldn't be having dinner with me. I got the distinct feeling that she was hesitant to say why, but when I asked her, she was honest.

"I'm having dinner with your father," she admitted.

There was something in her eyes. It only took me a moment to realize what it was: loneliness.

Her stance was on the sheepish side. "I know I must seem like a hypocrite to you. But I just realized recently that I do still kind of care for him. No. I take that back. Not kind of. I do care for him."

Not really sure how to respond to this little surprise, I said, "It's your life, Mom. We all have to make our own choices. But I really never thought I'd hear you say that."

My hand was resting on the checkout desk, and she laid her hand on mine. "Neither did I, dear. But watching him preach and seeing how so many people look up to him and depend on him, I guess I kind of began to see his side of things."

Oh my God! I thought to myself. And I'm sure I looked just as shocked.

She spoke up immediately. "I'm not saying that I was wrong all those years, Brenda. I'm not saying I was wrong in leaving him."

"Then, what are you saying?"

"That there are two sides to every story, I guess." She shook her head positively. "Yes! That's it. I am beginning to see his reasons now. That's all."

"I'll be honest, Mom. I think you're an idiot. But it's your life."

I know my words cut kind of deep. She looked really hurt, but just bobbed her head. "I guess I can't blame you for that." She sighed and looked around before turning back to me. "Maybe we can have dinner tomorrow night?"

"Maybe."

With a nod, she walked out.

At that moment, anger wasn't exactly what I felt. Betrayal was a much more accurate description. I know my eyes teared, but I refused to give in to the hurt. I loved my mother, but she wasn't as strong, and wasn't as committed as I had believed. One of the things that had been helpful in keeping me going the past few months was in knowing how strong I believed her to be with her convictions. She had kind of been my idol. The one I looked up to. Now that image of her had been smashed to smithereens.

Once I was in my car the tears began to leak. I went straight home, rushed inside and locked my door. I tossed my purse on the sofa and ran to my room and flung myself across my bed and let the damn of hurt and tears burst forth.

I'm not sure how long I laid there in my somewhat numb state. I know I drifted in and out of sleep several times. At one point I almost got out of bed to go shower and change clothes, but then I remembered that I had the following day off and just closed my eyes and tried to go back to sleep. I am not sure what time it was, but I believe it was some time after midnight.

I turned over on my right side and laid my left hand beside my head. A few moments later something feathery gently touched my forearm. At first I thought it might be Cal possibly desiring to cheer me up. I expected to be tickled in some way, but it didn't happen. Then the warmness slowly made its way down to my hand and rested there. That was when the incredible warmness enveloped me from behind. I turned my head just enough to see a bluish glow.

"I'm sorry I didn't make it back to you sooner," Paleo said in his husky but sweet timbre.

I turned the rest of the way over and gazed into his resplendent blue eyes. "I have missed you so!"

"And I, you! This last battle that I and my unit engaged in has lasted several days. In fact, it is still ongoing. I was beginning to think I wouldn't see you again for some time. But I felt your distress and hoped that Father would release me so that I might come to you… And He did."

"Thank you, Father!" I said and looked ceiling-ward.

Paleo's eyes twinkled. "He heard you."

"He is so awesome!"

"Agreed, my sweet." He peered into my eyes and I swear that I could see the stars there. Then he kissed me oh so wonderfully.

Until then, he had only made love to me from behind, and I had assumed that maybe that was how incubi always made love, but I had thought wrong. For I sensed something so incredible fill me that it took me a second to realize that he was making love to me as he faced me. I gasped in ecstasy, and we had not come anywhere near climax.

I had the awesome privilege of gazing into his perfect, glittering face that shone like myriads of brilliant gems, while he carried me to unimaginable, windswept heights, thousands and thousands of light-years away from all the pain and burdens of the world. Every now and then, he kissed my face in varied places: my nose, my cheek, my forehead and then my lips. With each kiss as gentle as a baby's caress. My love, my desire, for him knew no bounds. I wondered if all of his kind was as magnificent as he.

As always, he knew my thoughts; heard them as though spoken verbally. "We pride ourselves on being lovers of the ultimate kind, no matter who we mate with. But, I will tell you a secret, when we truly care about the one we mate with; we can surpass even our own expectations."

Is he saying he loves me?

"Yes!" he replied. "That is what I am saying. I love you, Brenda!" His statement was immediately followed by the most passionate surge that I could never have imagined. I think I glowed with him.

I was vibrating. I had become accustomed to a certain amount of vibration being around demons for a while now, but this vibration was rising rapidly. He was coming to climax, and my body and soul shared the spiraling rapture. All of a sudden I was shaking so hard that I thought surely I would explode. He tightened his grasp on me then, just as we climaxed together in what could have been a nuclear blast from all I sensed. I trembled helplessly in his powerful arms as I gazed into those resplendent eyes. I could see his love for me now, and knew that I loved him as well.

"Brenda," he whispered quietly.

This time I knew what he wanted to convey, for I felt it too. We were one together, complete, and would love one another for all eternity.

Afterwards, he held me lovingly in his arms for the longest time. Just being next to him was the most wonderful feeling. I knew that I would never be happier than when I was with him. Exhausted but in such a wonderful way, I fell to sleep in his embrace.

The next thing I knew it was morning and Paleo was gone. I understood that he had to get back to his duties, but I was thankful to Father for allowing Paleo and me to have the night together, and I said it aloud. "Thank you so much, Father!"

Then I heard as clear as a bell in my head, "You are more than welcome, Brenda."

There was so much on the news of war in the Middle East and elsewhere; conflict after conflict arising here and there. With the physical world in so much turmoil, I knew the spiritual was equally so. I also understood the importance of my lover's duties and didn't begrudge it at all when he couldn't come see me. But when we were together, all the time awaiting to be together fled away, and we spent each precious moment sharing our love and appreciation of the time we did have.

I considered us lucky if we had three nights a week together. However, it had gotten to the point that sometimes it was a week before he could return. I spent the rest of my time at my job or when home, meditating and studying. I tried to not waste one single moment when Paleo was not with me. By keeping occupied it helped the time to pass quicker, and I did my best not to linger on when he would be able to return. I knew he would return to me as soon as he could; knowing that made all the difference in the world.

Chapter Fifteen

With the exception of church nights, Mom and I still had dinner together almost nightly. The both of us went out of our way not to bring up our last argument.

I couldn't help but notice that she didn't mention Dad anymore either. In fact, she rarely said anything about church, but I knew she was going. She had a habit of sticking the church pamphlets and fliers in the open side-pocket of her purse, especially on Sundays. And when I had Sunday's off, she always came by around one, and was always dressed nice.

It was a little after one when Mom rang my doorbell. I had been expecting her, even though she hadn't called. It was pretty much an accepted thing anymore. I always gave her my schedule ahead of time, so she knew what Sundays I was home.

She stepped inside wearing a red pants suit that suited her honey blonde hair and green eyes.

"You look really nice," I commented. And she did, even nicer than usual.

"Why thank you, hon." She sniffed her nose. "Pot roast?"

"Yes. Was hungry for a good roast, mashed potatoes, carrots, the whole nine yards. I figure that even if you didn't show up, I could eat on it all week. Sandwiches, stew, what have you."

"I will be glad to help you. I love roast beef sandwiches."

"I know, Mom." I pulled out a chair for her at my little table. "Take a seat."

"Don't you want me to help you with anything?"

"I've got it covered. All done except for pouring our iced tea. Besides, isn't that a new pantsuit you're wearing?"

"Yes it is." Her eyes lit up. "Glad you noticed."

"It is red, Mom."

She grinned. "That it is. And I can get the tea."

"All right then. If you insist?"

"I do," she replied and got out glasses and filled them with ice for us and sat them on the table. Then she went to the refrigerator and took out the jug of tea and poured it.

Dinner ready, I loaded the roast and trimmings on a platter and placed it in the center of the table. Mom grabbed our plates and silverware.

We sat down and Mom bowed her head. She asked me if I wanted to say the blessings. I declined and said that she could. But I quietly thanked Father Satan for my dinner while she gave her thanks in her own way. What she didn't know wouldn't hurt her.

About midway through our meal, Mom laid her hands in her lap and looked at me as though there was something she wanted to say.

"Out with it, Mom," I said and dabbed my mouth with a napkin. "Whatever it is that's on your mind, just say it."

"Ah... I'm not sure how to put it without looking completely like a fool to you."

I knew. She didn't have to say it. I had seen it coming. "You're going back to Dad."

Surprised, she faltered briefly. "...Yes. How did you know?"

"I could see the signs. Doesn't take a genius to figure out how lonely you are. And the fact that you said you understood his side in our last little disagreement told me plenty."

"I have set him straight, Brenda. I want you to know that."

My first thought was a flippant response, but I stifled the urge. I wanted to say, "Sure you did." But I didn't. "Okay," was what I really said. My face must have given me away though.

"You don't believe me, do you?"

"Honestly... I believe that you believe you've set him straight. But I don't believe for one nanosecond that you have."

Hurt, she glanced off and got very quiet.

"I am not trying to hurt you, Mom. Nor am I trying to be glib: I know you know Dad... So just tell me exactly what rules or whatever you did lay down to him?"

"That I wasn't going to be his slave, for one."

"Go on," I said, thinking that that would be interesting to see.

"I let him know I would be there for him and the church. However, he has to spend some quality time with me every week. He has to take me to dinner or a movie, or just spend an evening with me at least once a week, at home or otherwise, that we need to have our time together as man and wife and not just for sex."

"Sounds reasonable." I did hope for her sake that he would. "And he agreed?"

"Yes! He did. He said he'd had plenty of time to think about our marriage while I was gone. He said he realized that he had neglected me something awful." She broke into a smile then.

"And you believe he meant it?"

She eyed me strangely, but replied, "Yes! I do believe him."

"Good. I really do hope he doesn't disappoint you, Mom. I really do!"

"I don't think he will," she said with conviction. "In spite of everything… in spite of his often blind absorption in the church, I do believe he loves me. In fact," she said with her smile turning into a big grin, "he wants us to renew our wedding vows in front of the whole congregation. Brenda, he wants us to get married all over again!" Her eyes danced then with little lights. It kind of tugged at my heart. This meant a lot to her.

I swallowed the urge to dispute her, afraid that my mother was being delusional about what was the true picture here, but I did not want to fight with her anymore. She was determined. I knew by now that people have to follow their own paths, whether they are right or wrong. "If that's what you really want, Mom? Then I will try to be happy for you."

"Oh, Brenda!" She stood and came over to me, throwing her arms around me, hugging me from behind. "Thank you!"

"For what?"

"For trying to understand. I know you don't fully believe it, but thank you anyway."

"I do believe I understand, Mom. You have to do what you feel you have to do."

She kissed my cheek and went back to her seat. I could see she was really pleased with my acceptance of her renewal of her marriage to Dad. I really had deep forebodings about it, but I knew she had to do what she felt she had to do. She had been there and done that, and if she hadn't learned her lesson yet, there was nothing I could do.

We finished off our supper and cleared off the table, and then she helped me load the dishwasher and put everything away. We went to the living room then to sit and talk.

She spoke first as she sat down. "Tell me, Brenda… Do you think that you might ever want to go back to Greg?"

I also had kind of foreseen this coming too. "No, Mom."

"But he loves you so much?"

I let out a disgruntled sigh and said, "I am happy for you. At least, I am happy that you are doing what you feel you want to do. However, even though I believe that in many ways Greg is a more pleasant individual than Dad, when it comes to getting along with him, I do not love him the way I used to. And way too many things have changed for me since I left him." Of course, I had Paleo in the back of my mind. I truly loved him and knew I would never be complete with anyone else now.

Mom leaned back and studied me for a bit. She finally spoke again, "Want to expound on some of those things?"

"You already know that I no longer believe the way you, Dad, and Greg do."

"But you do believe in God?"

Why did I bring that up? "We had an argument the last time we broached this subject, Mom. I shouldn't have said anything. Please, I don't want to fight with you again."

"Just tell me you believe in something. Please!"

I shook my head vigorously. "Yes! I do! I am very spiritual, Mom. You have no idea."

"Then explain some of it. Can you do that?"

"I think I mentioned it before. I lean towards Hinduism." It was the closest thing I could think of. After all, Satanism is Hinduism in its truest, original form.

She rubbed her neck with her hand and dropped her hand down. "Okay… Not what I would prefer to hear, but at least you have faith of some kind. You're not telling me you're an atheist."

"And I'm not! I love my God more than you will ever know!"

"Want to tell me what you call this God?"

"Mom!"

"If you are as spiritual as you say you are, can't you at least tell me his name? Or is it her?"

"He, Mom. My God is a he."

She wasn't going to back down. "Give me a name, please?"

She wasn't going to give up. "Okay… His true name is Ea. However, he later became known as Enki… And Ea is pronounced Arya, by the way." There was no way I was going to tell her that he was now known by the name of Satan.

She nodded as though considering my words. "Okay."

I could see the wheels turning in her head. "You asked and I told you. Please don't go running to Dad and telling him. Please!"

After several moments of musing, she said, "Okay. I know he would have a hissy fit for you believing in anything other than the way you have been raised. I know he's never completely gotten over the Wicca thing."

"Actually, neither have I," I mumbled under my breath, and then replied, "but thank you, Mom."

"Arya," she mused. "Is that where the word Aryan comes from? Like the Aryan race?"

"Yes. He is blond with blue eyes."

"Oh?" Her expression was dubious to say the least. "You actually know what he looks like?"

"I haven't seen him exactly… But this is what I have learned about him." I came very close to saying He is the father of mankind, but I knew that would stir her up, and I wasn't in the mood to deal with it. Right at that moment, though I had no doubts whatsoever that Mom loved me, I considered her possibly dangerous if she were to tell Dad. I had probably already said way too much. Even with good intentions, she was known not to think things through before acting on them.

"You wanted to know. I told you."

"Yes you did. And I appreciate it." She offered me a warm smile, but I seriously questioned the validity of it, and as to whether I could really trust her with my revelations. I hoped that I could.

"Surely there is some literature I can read up on this – Arya?"

"Sumerian, Mom."

"Oh?"

I quickly changed the subject and asked her about her job. Did she still like it? I let out a sigh of relief. She took the bait. Or maybe she didn't really want to fight either. I was glad it worked.

Though tired when she got off of an evening, she liked the doctors and other staff members. I was just happy to get her focusing on something else. I had the feeling that it wasn't going to end here, though. I love my mother, but she doesn't always use her head. And I had taken a real chance on telling her as much as I had.

*

A couple of weeks passed and nothing had resulted due to what I had told Mom. I hoped that she did understand how important it was that she didn't tell Dad all I had confessed to her.

Paleo had come to me several times, and our love-making was just as wonderful as ever. In fact, it seemed to be more splendid each time he took me in his arms.

I missed him terribly when he didn't come, but I also was happy to know that he would return to me as soon as he could. Just knowing I had him in my life made all the difference in the world.

I was so thankful to Father Satan for Paleo. Father was so good to me. I can't explain it where anyone can really fathom the depths of the love I have for Father. The difference being is that He is real! He loves his family! He takes care of us, and in ways that never cease to amaze me. And not only that, He sees to it we receive many blessings that we aren't even expecting. I shake my head in wonderment often. He is so thoughtful. Even when He is as busy as He is, He still takes the time to do the little things for us. He truly is a loving God!

Knowing how truly good Father is and how much He loves us, I often get upset when I am reminded of all the filth and lies that are continuously being spread about Him and His wonderful demons. I hate it when I come across a drawing of a red monster with horns, holding a pitchfork in his hands, or a depiction of someone's horrible rendition of a demon, especially an incubus or succubus. Some depictions are so monstrous that they could frighten grown men. Ridiculous! All the demons I have met or ever encountered briefly are either the most beautiful beings one could ever feast their eyes on, or they are the cute, spunky little dwarves like my friend, Cal.

What people don't consider: demons and angels are the same beings. It's kind of like politics. We have republicans and democrats in the United States. Well, in the supernatural world, we have demons and angels. Same species, just opposite sides of the fence!

There is no reason to think that Father Satan aka Ea-Enki is any less beautiful then he was in the very beginning! If only people would think for themselves. There are a few who do, but not many. Most folks blindly go where they are told to go, and just as blindly believe what they are told to believe.

One of Father's main things He tells his family: Question everything!"

There are so many people out there plagued with guilt over things they should not have any guilt for. Sex is the life-force of all creation! It is not something ugly! It is beautiful and to be cherished! Being a woman is not something to be ashamed of. We don't need to hide our faces! We don't need to hide our legs! And why not wear pants? They are far more comfortable than skirts and dresses and so much easier to move around in. Father loves us! He made us! We are His children biologically. We carry His DNA within our bodies!

At the same time, we women should respect what Father has given us. We should honor our bodies, and not dress in a manner that is deliberately, overly, enticing, unless it is for a desired mate. Still we can and should take pride in looking our very best, for ourselves and for our own sense of well-being.

I can't help it. I get really upset when I come across the lies that face us daily. I wonder that Father can be such a gentle and loving God in the face of all the lies that are constantly being said about Him. Still, He remains the most wonderful being anyone could ever know.

I had been rearranging some books on the different religions and mythologies of the world and stopped to browse through one I had not noticed before. It was about Jesus, and was written by Acharya S aka D.M. Murdock. I had already read several of her books and knew them to be well-researched and written. I thought I might check it out later. She is just one of many scholars I had read over the past year while learning the truth about Father. I do not believe she is a Satanist, but she is known to be very thorough in researching the truth.

Miranda called my name. A long line had formed in front of her. She was swamped. She indicated with a nod to three girls and a couple of boys of middle-school age standing in the back of the line. I rushed over and had the school kids form a second line.

*

It was a quiet and lazy Monday afternoon, and I happened to have the day off, so I strolled down to my friends' apartment. Paul was home working at his computer, but Nancy was at work. He seemed glad to see me and said he needed an excuse to take a break.

I took the easy chair, and he grabbed coffee for the both of us.

"So," I said, "how are things?"

"Great! Just got a direct deposit of a little over a thousand dollars for another special website I was building."

"That's good. I remember. You told me about it here a while back."

"Yep. I did. Finished it last week. Joe was more than happy with it, and threw in an extra hundred bucks."

"That is so awesome!"

He grinned slightly, turning his hooded eyes up to me. "It never ceases to amaze me the little extras Father gives us."

I knew exactly what he was talking about. "Yes. Exactly. There are a lot of folks who would say it was coincidence. But we know, don't we?"

He nodded, agreeing. "Yes! Happens far too often for it to be coincidental. Father loves us, and doesn't mind letting us know it."

"It's simply awesome!" My thoughts went to my mother then, and Paul picked it up.

"I take it something is bothering you?"

"My Mom."

"Oh? I thought you two were getting along?"

"Honestly, I think she's lost her freakin' mind. Can you believe that after all she has gone through… all the years of being miserable with that controlling, hypocritical, self-righteous father of mine, she is going back to him?"

"Say what?" He sat forward. Interest piqued. "Seriously?"

"You heard me right. She told me she'd had plenty of time to think things over and could now see more clearly from Dad's perspective. Not exactly in those words, but you get my drift. She also told me that there were terms in their getting back together – That he would have to set aside special time for her every week."

"I guess if he will do it, that it might possibly work… For a while, anyway." He grinned at me knowingly. "I seriously doubt it though."

"Knowing my father – the man who thinks he's God's gift to mankind – he will try for a while, maybe even for several months, but he is too set in his ways. And he's also much, much too absorbed in his duties to his church. I know he will always put his God and church first."

He took a sip of his coffee and set his cup on the coffee table. "I hate to see it, Brenda. I know you were so happy to have your mother back in your life. And I am sure you won't be able to have that closeness so much if she's going back to your father."

"I know. What really makes me sick: She finally got the courage to leave him. Has a job and can take care of herself, and she could easily find another man."

"She's probably scared, Brenda. She's how old – forty?"

"Forty-two on her next birthday in January."

"She may have had a chance or two with someone else while she was gone, but they didn't work out for some reason or the other."

"She's still too ingrained with her 'Christian' upbringing. There was this guy that she went to the movies and a dinner with once, but felt so guilty when she got home that she couldn't sleep that night. The next day she phoned him and told him she couldn't see him anymore."

Paul chuckled at the absurdity of it all. "What can I say? Too bad."

"Exactly! All that effort to better her life wasted."

"You know. I truly believe that it is that old codependency thing. She is so used to being controlled by her husband with a god-complex that she is afraid not to be. It's all she really knows."

"I hate to say it, but I think you are probably right. That is what I was thinking."

We talked for a little while longer and then Paul asked me if I wanted to run to Baskin Robbins with him to see Nancy. That he would buy me an ice cream cone.

I said sure, and he took us down in his truck. Just as we headed in the door – Paul held the door open for me – Greg walked out! The look on his face when he saw me with Paul was that of complete shock. Then his eyes went directly to Paul's necklace with the sigil of Satan. Instantly he looked at me, mouth agape.

Seeing this, Paul all but pushed me on inside, leaving Greg out on the walk just staring in at us. Something told me that this was only the beginning.

"Sorry about that," Paul said, as we went up to the glass case where the ice cream display was.

Nancy had witnessed the whole thing. "Oh my god!" she exclaimed, eyes huge.

"I'm really sorry about that, Brenda," Paul said, full of concern. "I know by his face what he thought."

"Me too. He probably thinks you're my boyfriend. And I know he saw your necklace."

"Without a doubt."

"If he gives you any crap at all," Nancy said, "don't hesitate to call us."

"Don't worry. I won't." I knew my friends would be there for me, one hundred percent. But I also had my supernatural friends: Cal, for one. And then there was Paleo. He was often away, but I knew that if he knew I was in danger that he would be there as quickly as he could.

"I am really sorry," Paul said again, as we sat down to a small table in the back.

"You had no way of knowing, Paul. It's okay."

"Still, the look on his face – He's not going to let this go."

"I know. But you know what, that's his problem."

Nancy joined us then, as all the patrons had left. "Finally, a break," she breathed.

"You're working alone today?" I inquired.

"No. Mike just ran to the bank to make a deposit. He'll be back any second now."

She no sooner said it and Mike whisked in the door. He grinned teasingly. "Oh… I see what you do when I'm gone."

"She just sat down," I said in her defense.

"I figured. We're never this dead for more than a few minutes." He winked and hurried on to the back.

*

The last thing I ever wanted to do was to walk back into Dad's church – especially to watch my mother and father renew their marriage vows. However, Mom called me after I got home from work the next evening and pleaded with me to the point that I thought surely I would lose my mind, and I finally said yes, just to get her to shut up about it. I couldn't wait to get off the phone.

It wasn't merely the fact that they were renewing their vows – something I considered utterly ridiculous at this point – I was uneasy as to how Greg was going to react to having seen me with Paul. I know he saw Paul's necklace with the sigil, and I had been expecting to have Greg and my Dad tearing down my door that evening.

Only, it didn't happen.

Almost a week went by, and Saturday was fast approaching. They were to renew their vows around six in the evening. I had been scheduled to work, but Miranda let me off the rest of the evening. Said I could come in a couple of hours early on Monday, since I worked the afternoon shift then. Truthfully, I had kind of hoped she would give me an absolute 'no', but it didn't happen.

I ate a light, early dinner, showered and wriggled into new jeans and a red, long-sleeved top. I certainly wasn't attired in any fancy manner, but what I put on had never been worn and was clean. I did wear my pretty red pumps that matched my top.

The wedding wasn't a fancy affair, but the entire congregation had been invited. All the pews in the front half of the church were filled. I took a lonely one in the back.

Mom and Dad stood at the right front of the church talking to Greg. I took it that Greg was to perform the ceremony. He glanced at me and smiled strangely. I'm not sure I'd ever seen that look on his face before, but I did my best to dismiss it. Mom saw me then, waved and smiled happily.

Shit! I was filled with a mixture of disgust, apprehension and dismay. I was only there for Mom, and as I sat there with many of the parishioners glancing back at me here and there, I just wanted to run out of the building. I felt like an enormous hypocrite just sitting there, letting them stare at me like that. It hit me then that I did not have to do this to myself. It was Mom's choice to return to a relationship she was miserable in, not mine. Then Ruth Jamison turned her smug, cocky face my way and that did it. I jumped up and ran out of the church.

I thought I heard Mom call after me, but there was no way I was going to go back in there. Just because she hadn't been strong enough to find her own way, and had chosen to return to a marriage of enslavement and live a lie, didn't mean I had to suffer the crap that went with it. I was a grown woman. I had Father Satan, Paleo, and Cal. They were all I needed. With that thought, I held my head high as I strode briskly up the park walk.

Of course, someone could have come after me, but I believe they felt I wasn't worth it – considered me a lost soul. I knew better. And it was also too close for their scheduled ceremony. Dad wasn't going to put off getting Mom back to chase after their evil daughter. I chuckled at that thought as I approached the park bench and sat down.

The service was beginning with a hymn, of course. Afterwards, I heard Greg's voice. I felt kind of numb at that moment. Suddenly I was aware of someone approaching and was glad to see it was Erick. He had on jeans and a dark tee-shirt, looked black, but I wasn't sure in the soft glow of the streetlights. Nevertheless, he looked awesome.

It was as though he knew. He greeted me with a friendly smile and a nod and took a seat beside me.

"Evening," I said.

"Thought you might be here. They announced the wedding Sunday evening. I wasn't sure if you would attend or not."

So he does go when I'm not there. "I did go. But I suddenly realized that this is Mom's mess. I don't have to deal with it. She wants to suffer with a life of blind obedience to Dad, that's her problem. Not mine!

"Good for you!" he said, and laid an arm across the bench behind my head.

I wondered why he even went to church there when, apparently, he really didn't believe that way.

He must have read my thoughts. He grinned perceptively. "The church is close. I just started going there more out of curiosity than anything. Met you and kind of got interested in your little dilemma."

"Well, I don't know why. But you sure have been there for me. I can't tell you how much I appreciate your more than kind generosity: Spending the night in the car with me that one night, to name one."

"You were in dire need of help, and I was more than glad to do it."

I really appreciated his friendship, I did. But he was so mysterious. He seemed to know almost everything about me, but he managed to be evasive when it came to himself.

Again, he must have read or heard my thoughts. He suddenly jumped up, and said, "Good to see you, Brenda."

"You too!" I stared up at him confused as to his sudden hurry.

Smiling pleasantly, he dismissed himself with a cordial bow and two-finger salute, and then briskly walked off to my right.

"Oh well," I mumbled to myself. "He is such an enigma."

Suddenly Mendelssohn's Wedding March being played on the church piano found its way to my ears. "Seriously? You've got to be kidding me!" I wasn't the one playing the piano, and I knew Mom wasn't. I figured it had to be George Fontaine, the regular pianist, or Ruth Jamison, at the keys. She was the only other person in the church that was good enough at the piano to play for the wedding. Not everyone knows it, but every pianist has his or her own unique style of playing. And it sounded like Ruth's touch at the keys. "Crap!"

Everyone was lining up outside on the church's front steps. Soon as Mom and Dad appeared at the door, they were showered with rice. Aghast, I shook my head. I had seen enough. I took off running and didn't stop until I reached my apartment. I quickly opened the door, ran inside, slammed the door and locked it. I was out of breath from running so hard and shaking from emotions that I could not ever begin to describe. I began shedding my clothes before I even got to the bathroom. I just wanted to take a shower and go to bed.

I stopped at my bathroom door. The water was already running and a yellow towel placed neatly-folded by the sink for me. "What the?" Then I realized Cal was standing just to my right.

I was naked as naked gets.

Eyes shining brightly, he grinned hugely but bowed politely. "Enjoy your shower, Brenda." Then he vanished.

"Thank you! I think."

Muted laughter.

I couldn't help smiling to myself. He was a stinker, but he was an adorable one. I did really appreciate his thoughtfulness, even though he might have harbored a few of his own ulterior motives behind it.

Chapter Sixteen

I was glad to work the early shift the next day. I didn't want to think about Mom and Dad at all. Just wanted to focus the best I could on my job. I kept busy checking books out for folks, and when it was all clear, I would busy myself putting away returned books. Done with that, I pulled out the duster from the back. I know I didn't stop for several hours. Miranda noticed. She came up to me finally, tapping me on the shoulder. I turned questioningly to her. "Yes?"

"Take a break, Brenda." She nodded at the wall clock behind the main desk. "It is two pm! You didn't even eat lunch!"

"Oh!" I realized that my stomach was growling. Had been for a while, but I had been ignoring it. "I didn't realize..."

I hadn't told her everything. She wasn't overtly religious but she did believe there was some creative force behind the universe, and she had little use for religious zealots. She understood. It was in her eyes. "Don't let your mother's foolishness get you down, hon. Focus on your own life... your own happiness."

I was surprised. "How did you know? Did I tell you about Mom and Dad renewing their wedding vows?"

"Not exactly. But the church isn't that far. As you know, a lot of the parishioners frequent the library here. I hear things."

"I guess you do."

"Go take that break," she said with a supportive smile.

"I think I will. Thanks!"

She nodded, and I headed for the back room to get my sack lunch and a cup of coffee.

When I got off work, I went straight home. I didn't know what I was going to do with myself. Both Paul and Nancy were working at Baskin Robbins, and Mom wouldn't be coming by for dinner anymore. That thought was just beginning to sink in. I had not realized how much I had come to enjoy having my Mom back.

And now she had abandoned me – again!

At least, that is the way I felt. The first time I had stood by my dad when she left. Now, I had left him too, and she had gone back to him. Talk about freakin', twisted irony!

I went through the motions of making myself a peanut butter and lettuce sandwich. I didn't feel much like going to any trouble to feed myself. I poured a glass of milk and took my meager supper to my little table.

I wasn't halfway through my sandwich when there was a knock on my door. Not sure who it could be – I wasn't expecting Mom – I opened the door guardedly.

Mom!

All dressed up in a royal blue pantsuit and smiling as though nothing different had transpired in the last few days.

"Are you going to invite me in, Brenda? Or are you just going to stand there staring at me like you would a stranger."

I glanced around at the parking lot.

"Don't worry," she said, knowing who I was looking for. "Your father didn't come with me."

"Good thing. Because he is not welcome in my home!"

The flicker of hurt in her eyes didn't faze me. She was a hypocrite in my eyes, and had totally betrayed my trust.

"I guess you can't help the way you feel. Guess I can't really blame you either… considering."

At least, she was admitting it. "Yeah," I cryptically replied. "Considering.

She blew out air, now growing a little irritated with me. "Am I welcome?"

I stepped back so she could come in.

"Thanks!"

I motioned for her to take a seat on the sofa. I sat on it too, as far on the opposite end that I could.

"You didn't come to the ceremony," she said, gaze anticipatory for an explanation. For some crazy, insane reason, she just didn't really get it.

"Is that a statement or a question?"

"A statement, I guess. I thought you were going to come… Stay, anyway. You left almost the minute you arrived. I know you're not happy with me—. "

"That's an understatement," I tartly interrupted.

Her entire face contorted in a frown. "I fail to understand your obvious hostility, Brenda."

I couldn't help it. I burst out laughing at her ludicrous statement.

"What on Earth is so funny?"

"You are the epitome of a hypocrite, Mom!"

"I know I disappointed you… But I thought you would understand. Can you clarify for me?" Her eyes filled with tears.

I was aghast at the profound stupidity of her reasoning. "You preached to me for years about going to college and getting an education… Wanted a 'different' life for me. Didn't want me to be a 'slave' to my husband the way you were all those years. You wanted me to have something to fall back on – A career. And when I fell in love with Greg and wanted to marry him, what did you do? You left me, Mom! *You left me!"*

Her mouth gaped as she listened to my angry retort. She was speechless.

"I tried! Oh how I tried. It hurt, Mom! It hurt like nothing I've ever suffered before. But I eventually accepted it. I loved Greg so much, and I wanted to be a good wife. I thought he was different than Dad. And he is to a degree. But not enough. Women are still subservient slaves in his and Dad's eyes…. You want to know why I am so angry?"

"I knew that it must have looked a little… Well, I'm not sure how to say it. That I looked somewhat of a fool to come back. But I had tried it on my own. All I could get was a minimum wage job. I worked hard for months waiting on tables in a small café. I was exhausted! I don't have the education or training to get a better job."

"There are organizations that help, Mom. You could have received training. Probably on the job." I took a deep breath. "And what is the job you have now? Aren't you a receptionist for a doctor's office?" I thought about it a minute. "Or you were?"

"Still am." She closed her eyes briefly and swallowed and then opened her eyes again. "You're right. I could have done better maybe. But I missed you! And believe it or not, I missed your father."

"So, you really do still love him?" I was dubious, for I could not understand her returning to him except for security.

She was crying now. "Yes."

I grabbed a tissue from the box on the kitchen counter and handed it to her, and then plopped back down in my seat.

She thanked me and blew her nose into it. She went to get up to throw it in the trash, and I told her to just leave it on the coffee table. I would get it later.

"Okay."

"You love Dad?" I found it hard to believe. But I could see it in her eyes, in her face.

"Yes," she said again.

"Okay, Mom. I'm sorry. But you must understand my anger. You have to admit that you are the biggest hypocrite I have ever known."

She sniffled and nodded yes. "You're right. That I am. I'm sorry. But please know I never meant or wanted to hurt you the way I have. Brenda, you're my daughter. You're my only child. I love you!"

I stood. As angry and hurt as I was, I still loved my mother. I went over to her and sat down with her, giving her a hug. "I'm sorry, Mom. I just wish you would have explained it to be better first."

"I wanted to. I just didn't know how."

"I guess sometimes one has to get really upset and angry before they can really see their true feelings." I shrugged and took my arms back, leaning against the sofa.

"I've never thought of it that way before. But I think you're probably right."

I offered Mom a cup of coffee then, and she accepted. We managed to focus the subject to our jobs. I was glad we had cleared the air, but I still marveled how it was that she could have such a good job now that she was back, but she couldn't get one while she was away. I could only conclude that the truth really was like she said – that she just missed us and wanted to come home.

*

We were especially busy the next few days at the library. I barely had time to eat lunch and take a pee before I would have to get back up to the front desk or help someone on a computer.

It seemed that many middle school kids were working on special assignments for a number of teachers from a couple of schools. They all happened to want their projects in at approximately the same time. And to top it off, we had another book sale. I felt like a spinning top half the time, not knowing which way to go first.

To say I was glad to get Wednesday evening off is an understatement. Nancy was working, and Paul had another website to work on, and Mom, of course, was now caught up in the madness of being a preacher's wife again. Needless to say, she had little time for me anymore. And I wasn't surprised when she called me while she was out on an errand and told me she had quit her job at the doctor's office.

I hated to hear that. But I had pretty much expected it. Now she was the one doing errands and waiting hand and foot on two self-centered, self-righteous 'men of God'. I did not envy her, nor did I feel sorry for her. She knew what she was getting into when she went back to Dad. I just shook my head and pocketed my phone.

I just wanted to get what little house cleaning that was needed out of the way, and enjoy the rest of my day and evening off.

I had just started watching the series *Merlin* on Netflix and absolutely loved it. I had myself all worked up and anticipating watching two or three episodes before doing my nightly meditation, taking my shower and going to bed.

Paleo had paid me a visit the night before and had let me know that he probably wouldn't make it back for several nights. I wasn't crazy about not seeing him more than two or three nights a week, but I knew how it went. I was just thankful that he could spend as much time with me as he did. I had grown to love him so much! I can't explain it. I loved him as much or more than I ever could a human male.

He was all I needed and all I wanted when it came to a personal relationship.

Then there were the warm hugs from Father. One has to experience them to ever understand. Such love! He loves His children so much and doesn't mind expressing it. Every now and then, I would be in the kitchen standing at the sink washing dishes, or sitting on the sofa watching television, or putting clothes away, and I would suddenly feel this warm, soft and feathery sensation envelope me, similar to Paleo's hugs, and I sometimes have trouble telling the difference at first, but after a moment, I know by instinct. Father has never materialized as much as Paleo. And Paleo and I always end up making love.

Still, to have a hug from your loving God – There's nothing like it! Nothing!

I turned my television on, set it on Netflix, and brought up the second season of Merlin. I had a fresh cup of coffee and was all set to relax and just enjoy my private time watching television.

Then there was a loud knock on my door.

I wasn't expecting anyone, but I jumped up to answer it and just as I swung the door open, I heard Cal clearly in my head, "Don't open it, Brenda!"

Too late. Dad and Greg stood there with faces of marble. Several church deacons stood to their left, and there were more church members sitting in their cars in the parking lot. I could also see Mom in the back, teary-eyed and visibly shaken, but Rose was with her and appeared to be trying to comfort her. I could easily envision the scenario. Mom, in her somewhat unrealistic and childish way, had not thought things threw and had told Dad far too much. This definitely was not good. Not good at all! I attempted to slam the door, but Dad caught it and rudely pushed his way inside.

"You have no right barging in like this!" I angrily stated. "This is *my* home! Get out!"

"You are *my* daughter and Greg's wife!" Dad retorted. "And being men of God that makes you our business! You have fallen victim to the wiles of the devil. We tried to help you once, but you feigned cleansing. This time you will not fool us!"

I pushed, shoved, and fought them the best I could as they grabbed for me, but they were too many and too strong. The next thing I knew tape covered my mouth and someone slipped a sack over my head, and I was bodily carried out.

As they stuck me in the back of one of the member's van, I heard Mom whimpering how sorry she was. Dad told her she had nothing to apologize for.

"I'm not telling *you* I'm sorry!" Mom yelled back. But I think Dad ignored her remark.

Too late, Mom!

They didn't take me to Dad's church. Whoever was at the wheel just continued driving. Where were they taking me? I soon realized our destination was out of town. I figured they had something not quite right up their sleeves. Otherwise, why would they bother to take me so far? Maybe they were afraid the police might interfere if things got too crazy at the church.

When the van finally stopped and I was carried out, other than the parishioners' cars pulling in, I realized there were few traffic sounds.

They carted me into a building, but from the acoustics, I realized it wasn't a church, or even a regular building. It had to be a large garage or barn of some kind.

The sack was removed and the tape ripped from off my mouth. It was dark at first, but then lights began to come on one by one. It took me a few minutes, but I recognized the building, as we had passed by it many a time through the years, when we took family excursions out of town. The building belonged to Deacon Ted Randolph, but from what I understood it hadn't been used in years. I could remember overhearing him ask Dad years ago if he was interested in buying it. Dad had said he'd think about it. That he could possibly use it for big revivals.

Mom ran up just then, with Ruth tugging at her arm attempting to pull her back. "Don't do this, Robert! Please!"

"Gale," Dad stated with determination, "you just told me this evening how worried about her you are. That she admitted she didn't worship God."

"Our God," Mom corrected.

"Gale! Don't! This has to be done!" His eyes went to Greg, who was looking every bit as determined as Dad now. "And Greg here has been working up the nerve to tell me Brenda is seeing Satanists!"

"I think they're just her friends," Mom mumbled, but then the look on her face revealed that she realized saying that had been a mistake too.

Dad just looked at her in angry dismay.

They set me on my feet and Greg stood in front of me, eyes full of the same crazed fierceness that was in Dad's.

One of the deacons handed a Bible over to Dad. Immediately, Dad began spewing out scripture upon scripture. I just stared at him. The only feelings I had for him now were cold hatred and rage at his stupidity. This ridiculous prattling of scriptures went on for twenty minutes or more, while Mom stood in the background sniffling and looking very worried. And when she did look at Dad, there was something new there – hate. It was obvious she realized she had made a huge mistake in renewing her wedding vows.

I almost laughed when Ruth approached her again as though to comfort her and Mom told her to keep her freakin' hands off. Shocked, Ruth stepped to the far side of the men, looking at Mom as though she were possibly possessed.

"You're not getting anywhere," Greg interrupted after a bit.

Dad stopped then, eyes shining like a madman's, and glued to my face. "You're right, Greg. Has to be a powerful demon. I was afraid we'd have to resort to extreme measures, and it appears we have no choice."

Nodding that he thought Dad right, Greg ran out of the barn.

"What do you mean?" Mom yelled as she ran up. "What extreme measures?"

"We have this under control, Gale! Let Greg and me handle this!"

Ruth stepped closer in, eyes afire. She was drinking in every moment as though it were some wonderful show that she wouldn't miss for the world.

Greg dashed back in with a blanket and ropes.

"What are you doing?" Mom asked, hysteria growing in her voice.

Dad turned to one of the other deacons then and told him to get Mom out.

"No!" Mom pleaded. "No! No! No!" But she was dragged out by a couple of men. I could hear her screaming in protest, but no one was heeding her pleas. Then silence. Apparently she was locked up in a car and her mouth taped over too.

Ruth's grin grew bigger. At that moment, I could have beat her to a pulp had I been able to get my hands on her.

With the help of the two deacons, Dad and Greg wrapped the blanket tightly around me, with it coming up to my chin. I could barely breathe, it was so tight. That wasn't enough for them. They secured three ropes around me: one at my ankles, one at my waist, and the third around my shoulders. Not only could I barely breathe, I was so hot I thought I would pass out.

They laid me down on another blanket and once more Dad began his ridiculous sputtering of scriptures. When I could stand it no longer, I screamed, "I hate you! I will hate you until the day I die!"

At that, Greg joined in the preposterous blathering. I had to do it. I was so freakin' pissed and miserable. I spit in Greg's face. I wish I had had a camera to capture his shocked expression. It was priceless. I don't know why he was surprised. It wasn't the first time I had spit in his face, and for the very same reason. He simply froze for a few seconds, and then, apparently, decided it was the demon that made me do it. Idiot!

What they didn't know was that Satan's demons don't enter into a human body unless invoked, requested, by that individual to do so. And it is usually to aid in that person gaining certain knowledge, help them in some way. They never – and I mean never – do the vile things that books and movies portray! That is all fiction! All lies! They are powerful beings – yes! But they are loving and faithful to Father Satan's children. They would never harm one. Never!

Dad and Greg kept on and on and on. They either didn't care or were too caught up in their rambling, to notice that I was having trouble breathing, seriously, now. It was all I could do to remain conscious.

"This is not working," Dad stated and handed his Bible to one of the deacons. Give me your belt, Greg."

Greg looked startled, but Dad stubbornly held out his hand. Then nodding okay, Greg quickly undid his belt and handed it over to Dad. That was when Dad began to lash me with the belt – buckle ended. I cried out. And I guess the blankets protected me somewhat, but Dad was hitting me as hard as he could and demanding the demon to come out of me. I suddenly felt like I was going to throw up. Too hot. Sick. I strained my neck to turn my head the best I could. Then a woman yelled that I was throwing up, to sit me up so I wouldn't choke.

Greg quickly sat me up, and I threw up in his lap. It would have been hilarious had I not been so freakin' sick.

Then, I thought I saw a shadow slip behind Ruth. A short shadow. Then a familiar face – Cal!

And was he pissed!

Suddenly, Deacon Randolph yelled out as he sailed over an old John Deere tractor that had been behind him. Then Ruth turned and met the fury in Cal's red eyes and screamed, as he focused his ferocity on her. She scrambled out of the building with Cal at her feet.

"What is going on?" Dad asked, as he and Greg whipped their heads around to see what was happening. "We need to focus here! Can't afford distractions!" The self-righteous bigots realized then that Deacon Randolph was lying on the dirt floor on the far side of the tractor, rubbing the back of his head.

Some of the other church members quickly left out the side door, but the rest hadn't seen what had happened and were too engrossed in watching the exorcism. Myself, I had a front row view, making it almost worthwhile.

Dad and Greg eyed one another. Dad told Greg to go over and see about Randolph. Then Dad turned to me and raised the belt back to lash out at me again. Just then, there was a crack of thunder, so loud that it startled everyone. Then there was a slight trembling of the ground. Dad lost his balance and fell backwards. Deacon Bill Phillips helped Dad up and to brush off. Dad refused to be deterred, though, pulling his arm back and then hit me with all the fury he could muster.

There was another, even louder, crackle of thunder, and the ground shook even harder, and this time it didn't stop. Kept shaking.

Someone yelled we were having an earthquake.

"No!" Dad stubbornly protested. "Just proof she has a powerful demon in her! It's trying to stop me from saving her. But he's not going to succeed!" And he slapped the belt across my chest as hard as he could. "In the name of Jesus, I command you to come out, demon!"

Then all the lights shut off, and a murmuring went around through the church members who still remained. Another loud rippling of thunder rolled overhead.

"Don't let it frighten you," Dad said, hoping to calm everyone.

Then a huge ball of light, soft at first, began forming right behind Dad. Greg noticed it immediately and yelled at Dad to look.

Dad turned around to see and had to squint, for the light was now blinding. Then, barely detectable at first, a form appeared in the light, a very impressive, tall figure of a man. He had to be at least seven feet tall. Dad gasped. Then the bluish white form stepped forth out of the light and I recognized him immediately: Paleo in full armor! It was the first time I had ever seen his beautiful shimmering physique fully formed and standing, but I knew him by the shape of his head and the way he moved.

There was another loud crack of thunder and the lights came back on, and the ball of light that Paleo had stepped out of dissipated.

Dad stood a little askew to me. His jaw hung loose and his eyes couldn't have been any bigger, as Paleo swiftly strode up to him, grabbed him by the collar, raising him high in the air with one arm, while Dad kicked his feet, trying desperately to free himself, and then Paleo slung him across the barn. Dad hit the wall, feet up, with a loud thud. I thought surely he was dead, but I heard him moan. Paleo turned then to Greg, who was backing away with his Palms up. "No! Please! No!"

"This is how you treat your wife?" Paleo asked in a feral snarl.

"I'm sorry! I'm sorry!"

"That you are." Paleo's gaze went to Dad then, as Dad had managed to pull himself up to a sitting position. But he wasn't looking too good.

"You'd be wise to stay there," Paleo warned.

Dad shook his head, terrified. He wasn't about to move. Many of the onlookers who weren't frozen to their spots turned and scrambled out of the building.

Paleo turned his attention back to Greg, and Greg screamed as Paleo lifted him up and threw him across the barn too. Deacon Phillips and the other deacons tried to flee, but Paleo was too quick. They all went flying one by one, landing with thuds against the barn walls.

With the church people out of the way, Paleo quickly untied me and scooped me up in his arms. "I'm sorry I didn't get here quicker, my love, but it took Cal a few minutes for his message to get to me and hone in to where you were."

I looked up at him with the greatest love. My eyes were full of tears, but not from pain. My heart sang with joy just to behold him. And he had rescued me! "I love you!"

Adoring me with his wonderful eyes, he smiled and kissed my cheek. "I love you too, my sweet."

Shaking visibly, Dad managed to pull himself to his feet, as so did Greg. Some of the deacons were still sitting, too terrified to move a muscle.

Face contorted in confusion and fear, Dad finally got brave enough to ask, "Are you an angel?"

"Same species… different side of the fence," Paleo curtly replied.

Mom stepped back inside then. Cal was beside her. Apparently he had freed her. When she saw me in Paleo's arms her face lit up in awe. Speaking to Paleo, she gasped, "You're beautiful!"

That brought on a polite smile from Paleo. Then he returned his attention to Dad and Greg. "For your information, I am what you would refer to as a demon."

Dad gulped audibly.

"Contrary to the lies taught by your kind, we demons are *not* monsters. If truth be known, we are actually gods in our own right. And we do not cause or make you humans do anything wrong, evil or otherwise. Man commits acts of violence and evil all on his own volition."

Dad's eyes grew bigger and bigger as Paleo spoke, but he dared not interrupt.

"If you want to place blame on someone, then blame the ones on *your* side. They have led you to believe their lies for thousands of years. It is your God who would have mankind enslaved, and has taught you that everything normal and natural is evil. It is all a lie! You, sir, do not teach the truth. The Jews, Christians, and Muslims have all developed unnatural faiths on the claimed God of the supposedly chosen Jews, along with a combination of other beliefs and much fabrication of facts!"

Dad and Greg were both utterly speechless. Dad then looked over at Mom, who turned her face away from him. Then Dad focused back on Paleo. "My... My entire life has been based on a falsehood? I... I can't believe that," he stuttered. "It's all in the Bible."

Paleo laughed heartily before responding. "You imbecile, the proof is there for you to study. There are numerous books written by scholars who have researched the truth. The false religions have done their best to destroy and hide it, but it is still there."

"You say you are a demon," Dad said. "So why should I believe you?"

"Do you see an angel here rescuing your very-abused daughter?"

Dad glanced around at the others, they had no answer, and he looked back at Paleo but didn't respond.

Greg stepped forward, eyes on me, and then questioningly to Paleo, and then back to me. "I'm sorry, Brenda."

I could see he meant what he said. Only, my heart was now Paleo's, and I knew it would be forever. "I believe you, but it's too late, Greg. I'm sorry."

Greg nodded. Regret all over his face. "Not as sorry as I am." He grimaced and stepped back.

Suddenly, the earth shook again.

"Maybe that's an angel?" Dad sneered.

Paleo simply laughed.

Another light appeared. This time, I was the one stunned. For out of the light stepped a very familiar form. *"Erick?"* I felt Paleo's chest chuckle slightly.

This time Erick had brilliant white wings, and he was dressed in a robe of pure white. "That is the name I use sometimes when I want to help one of my children," he replied in a wonderfully kind voice. "I'm sorry that I had to temporarily deceive you, but I didn't want to let you know who I really was until I deemed it necessary."

Dad's face grew red. "Don't tell me you're Satan?"

Eyes temporarily afire with anger towards my dad, Father replied, "That I am! My true original name is Ea, pronounced Arya, but I have been known as Satan for many, many years now."

"But... you're dressed in white?"

Father shook his head. In spite of all he was witnessing, Dad still stubbornly clung to his engrained beliefs. Father turned his attention to me then, and stepped up to us. His eyes met Paleo's and they shook their heads as though speaking to one another telepathically. Then Father proceeded to unwrap me, and then Paleo set me to my feet, but held his arm lovingly around me.

Father said, "I am sorry you had to endure this, my child." He kissed my forehead and stepped back, turning his stare to my dad.

It was so obvious that Dad didn't want to believe any of this was happening, but many of the others were looking at him as though they felt sorry for him and then turned and started leaving. "Don't let yourselves be deceived!" Dad yelled after them.

Father spoke again and the ground shook. "Even now you deny me?" His wonderful blue eyes sparkled with ire.

Dad just stared at him and chewed his mouth around but didn't respond.

"I believe in you," Greg said. "I will never preach the lie again. I am willing to serve you, Lord Satan."

"Thank you, my child. You will receive my blessings and love for your faith."

Mom came forward and accepted Him too. Father took them both in his arms and hugged them lovingly. Then the few parishioners, who had remained, came forward and also dedicated to Father.

Dad just growled and stormed out of the building.

Father's eyes followed him. Then he looked at Paleo and sighed woefully. I could see it hurt Him deeply that my Dad refused to believe the truth, in spite of all he had witnessed. "Sadly, some are so deceived by the influence of the other side there is just no getting through to them."

Paleo agreed. "It is indeed sad."

Father then explained that He and Paleo needed to return to the war that still raged on the other side. Then he asked Greg if he could take me and Mom home.

"Of course," Greg replied. I could see he was aware there was something between Paleo and me, but he wasn't going to question it.

Father and Paleo vanished, and Greg led Mom and me out to his car. The rest left too.

Mom let Greg take her to the house, but also let us know that she wasn't going to stay. She thought she could get her old apartment back, and possibly her job. She had made a mistake in going back to Dad. That she regretted. She felt sorry for him, but there was nothing she could do about that.

Soon as Greg dropped her off, he took me to my apartment. We sat in the front seat for a minute. Things were playing on his mind. Then he turned to me and asked, "Do you love this Paleo?"

"Yes! I won't lie. He loves me too."

"I could see that… This is all so incredible. I would never have believed any of it had I not witnessed it personally. I do know Satan is our true Father now. And knowing that makes me happy inside in a way that I never was before."

This I understood completely. "Yes. Knowing the truth and having Father's love is the most wonderful thing that could ever happen to us."

He leaned over and kissed me lightly. "I know Paleo will take good care of you. But I will always love you, Brenda."

"I will always love you too, Greg. Just not the way I love Paleo."

"I understand that… I think." And he smiled regretfully.

"You will find someone. I am sure in Father's kingdom there is someone special for you."

"I don't doubt it."

He jumped out then and came around and opened the door for me. Then, with a quick hug, I dashed to my front door and let myself in. I stopped with a start.

Cal stood in my kitchen door, grinning like the Cheshire cat.

"What now?" I expected to see all my soda cans emptied and lined up along the counter, or find a bra hanging from the ceiling (something he actually did to me once), instead, he had a spaghetti and meatball dinner placed on the table for me, and iced tea poured in a tall glass. What's more, he had set himself a place as well.

"Dinner, my lady?"

"Cal! You sweet dear!" I kissed the top of his hooded head.

He pulled my chair out for me, and I took my seat.

He sat down too, and then watched intently as I took my first bite.

I couldn't believe it. "This is the most delicious spaghetti I ever tasted."

That brought on a huge grin. "Thank you, my lady!" he winked and began shoveling his dinner into his mouth as fast as he could. Red sauce dripped down his chin, but I kept my mouth shut and just watched him with amazement, astounded he could eat so fast. Suddenly there was a loud fart, and he grinned mischievously, but didn't apologize, and then there was another fart, followed by another, and then another, and then burping ensued, but he just smiled and kept stuffing his face.

I couldn't help it. I laughed and continued eating my delicious dinner.

The end

*This may be the end of my novel, and though the story is fiction, it is not the end. My story is founded on extensive research and studies.
However, for those of you who question the validity of things, the answers are out there. You just have to look for them.

There are numerous works by many scholars that one can read and study. Some of these fine scholars are:
Acharya S aka D.M. Murdock
Zecharia Sitchin
Robert Graves
James Frazer
Erich Von Däniken

The television series *Ancient Aliens* skillfully raises many of these questions.
There is more, much more. One only has to apply themselves if they want to know the truth.

Amber Geneva

ambergeneva@outlook.com

www.ingramcontent.com/pod-product-compliance
Lightning Source LLC
Chambersburg PA
CBHW070819120626
46556CB00002B/574